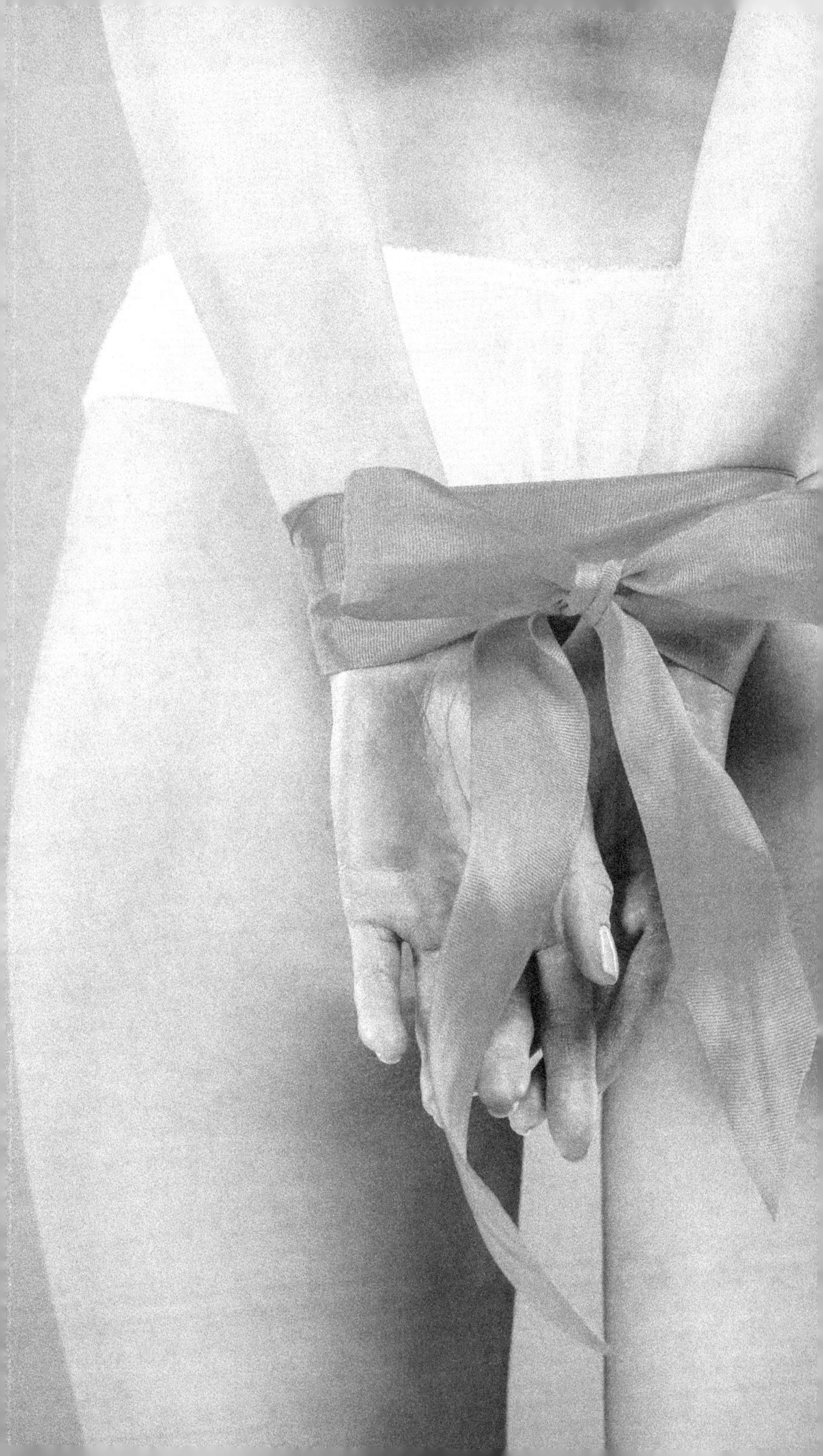

Christmas
CAPTIVE
USA TODAY BESTSELLING AUTHOR
ISABELLA
STARLING

CHRISTMAS CAPTIVE

"Christmas isn't a season. It's a feeling."

- Edna Ferber

Please refrain from spoiling this book for yourself or others.

DEDICATION

I am dedicating this book to every single member of my Facebook group!
You ladies motivate me day after day. You make every day brighter and every hour spent in your company puts a smile on my face. Thank you for encouraging me, having my back and holding my hand when I need it.
Merry Christmas, good girls!
Your Isa

PROLOGUE

Grayson

1 year ago

I fucking hated Christmas.

And that day promised to be even lonelier, now that Lyra had cancelled on me, telling me she had to attend a family dinner. I was pissed off. I wanted to finally fuck her that night, but she took that opportunity away from me. I knew I'd have to punish her for it eventually, and unfortunately for Lyra, I was looking forward to it very much.

Instead of spending the day in my playroom, I decided to pay a visit to Couture House. I'd received countless invitations from them, asking me to come to one of the infamous auctions they held in their building. Today, the Christmas auction would take place, and the most willing and most beautiful toys would be auctioned off to the highest bidder.

I got my toys from a variety of places—sometimes they were the daughters of a business acquaintance I particularly despised, sometimes they just fell in my lap—debutantes, heiresses, all those girls so very eager for a strong hand to put them in their place. My right hand man, Kai, had told me the December auctions at Couture House were especially important. That they saved their very best for them. I didn't want to get my hopes up, but I still found myself quite excited as I made my way to the building in Notting Hill.

Limos and expensive cars littered the street outside, my own joining their ranks. My driver opened the door for me, and I buttoned my blazer, heading inside the building to see whether the promises Couture House made held any value.

Inside, it was all suits and the scent of expensive cigar smoke. Someone asked for my drink preference, and not even a minute later, a tumbler appeared on a silver platter, proudly presented to me by a waiter. With my drink in hand, I was shown to my table— the very best in the room, as it should have been. It was right in front of the stage, giving me a wonderful view of everything that happened up there. Nothing would escape my watchful gaze here. I felt my cock hardening in my pants, excited for what was to come, and eager to plunge into the victim I would pick tonight.

Ever since Lyra cancelled on me, the annoyance I felt was palpable, reminding me that I needed to find a more permanent solution to my problem. I'd been toying with socialites for too long. It was time to found someone worthy of my attention, and possibly, my ring on her finger. But so far, the search for a future Mrs. Kline had been fruitless. I was a picky man, and I had peculiar tastes in my playthings which meant rarely any of the women I was presented with kept my interest for longer than a few days. Sure, I'd make them scream into my silk pillows. I'd make them never forget the name Grayson Kline. But at the end of the day, they were just distractions. A momentary reprieve from what I *really* fucking wanted.

A wife.

A mother to my children.

A capable, smart opponent who could match my smarts and my wit.

And someone who wouldn't think twice of kneeling for me and showing me how deeply she cared for me as her wet little mouth enveloped the thickness of my cock.

The auction was gearing up to start, and the rambunctious laughter in the room faded to excited whispers as the head of Couture House made his way onto the stage. He was handsome, around my age but leaner and not as broad-shouldered as I was. Still, I could imagine the girls here fawned over him.

They began bringing out the women. It was a cornucopia of stunning victim after victim, doe eyes wide with excitement and fear, bodies glittering with shimmering powder. Not one of them held my interest despite the fact that they were all painfully perfect. Perhaps that is exactly what bothered me about them— that there was no room for improvement. They were all already perfectly meek and obedient, and unfortunately, boring in their perfection.

I saw the girls notice me. It happened several times when their gazes wandered through the audience, probably wondering who their new owner would be. Their gaze caught mine, and I searched their innocent eyes for signs of what I wanted in a companion. Some of them were kinky, sure. I could tell from the way their bodies arched when they saw me, eager to get closer to me, eager to be beneath me as I pounded into their flesh without reservations. But the spark was missing. And the spark was important. More important than their silky legs and bare breasts with hardened, puckered rosy nipples.

I was getting more and more disappointed by the second, and I knew the girls could tell. One of them, a stunning blonde, stared me down for what felt like hours, trying to catch my attention. But it didn't work. I had no interest in a virginal, perfectly pretty little toy like her. I wanted more. I wanted... someone that wasn't here.

In the middle of the auction, I stood up, getting ready to leave the room. In moments, one of the employees of Couture House was standing by me, eager to prevent me from leaving.

"Something wrong, Sir?"

"I don't think I'll find what I'm looking for here," I muttered, eyes sweeping over the stage where a pretty redhead was being bid on. Still, her eyes lingered on me, hoping I'd raise my paddle to bid on her virginity. "These girls aren't exactly my type."

"Sir, if you tell us what you're looking for, we might be able to serve you better," the employee, a man in his early thirties, was eager to answer. "We pride ourselves on finding the perfect match for anyone and everyone. Would you like to fill out a form? Despite the fact that you didn't find someone suitable today, we might be able to accommodate you in the future."

A form. I chuckled at the thought. Who would have thought finding the perfect submissive would come down to filling a goddamn form. And yet I couldn't resist. I wanted this. Even the thin promise on the man's lips excited me. I gave him a curt nod, followed him to an office in the back, and stared at the form he presented me with.

It was detailed, demanding to know everything from the woman's hair color to her weight and age. But I didn't give a shit about any of that. I had a type, of course, but it had nothing to do with the girl's appearance, and everything to do with her delightful little brain.

Finally, I settled for writing a single line on the form.

I want a captive to keep over Christmas.

Smirking to myself, I handed the form to the perplexed employee of Couture House and headed out of the auction house. As I passed through the main room, I felt several pairs of eyes following me, including those of men whom I would never expect to see in a place like this. I nodded to a few acquaintances, pretended not to notice the two members of Parliament in the front row, and ignored the famous American actor and his wife who were scoping out a potential new victim.

But as I made my way to the exit, the sinking feeling of failure reminded me I was once again going home to an empty apartment.

I hadn't even decorated for Christmas. Anything to distract me from the boring, depressing truth—that I was more alone than ever.

I could have a slew of women at my apartment at the click of my fingers, and yet the thought didn't excite me. I wanted more than a random fling. For the first time in my life, I found myself wishing for more than a set of holes to fuck. I wanted a companion. Not a toy. Someone worthy of my attention, someone worthy of spoiling.

I pondered all this as my driver pulled away from Couture House and toward my penthouse apartment in London. The driver opened my door once we arrived, and I nodded at him, dismissing him as I slipped a fifty into his hand. I walked over the pavement to the glitzy lobby of the building I owned when something caught my attention.

Lyra, my would-be date was standing in the lobby, mascara smeared and her makeup ruined. The doorman dashed toward me just as she did.

"I'm sorry, Sir," the man rushed to get the words out. "She wouldn't take no for an answer, she was so desperate to see you, and I didn't know how to stop her."

"It's alright," I muttered. "But this can't happen again. Got it?"

He nodded in understanding just in time as the girl rushed toward us the next second, clinging to me with desperation.

"I'm so sorry I turned you down, Sir," she whispered, tears already falling down her perfectly pretty face. "The dinner was a disaster... My parents will never understand me. I didn't know where else to go, Sir... Are you angry that I'm here?"

I gently pried her fingers off my expensive suit, tucking a stray strand of hair behind her ear. "No, I'm not angry, but I don't have time for you right now."

The lie slipped from my lips easily, and Lyra's bottom lip wobbled at the words. "Please, Sir, I'll do anything, just don't make me go back home."

She had my interest now. Any time a woman promised everything, I got fucking excited. It meant I could push them to their very limits.

"Anything?" I wondered out loud, and she was quick to nod, so very eager it was almost laughable.

"I'm so sorry, Sir, please, let me make it up to you... I want to give you everything, please, let me show you how grateful I am."

I pondered her words for a beat too long, enjoying how nervous it made her to see me contemplating her fate.

"What do you want, Lyra?"

"To come upstairs with you," she begged. "Please, Sir..."

She attempted to touch me again, but thought better of it when she saw my annoyed expression. Quickly, she retrieved her perfectly manicured hands, bottom lip trembling with barely held back desire.

"You'll be a good girl for me?" I wondered out loud. "You'll do *anything* I fucking want, Lyra?"

"Of course, Sir," she purred. "Please... let me show you how sorry I am. Let me give you everything... Let me offer my body for you to take. You can do whatever you want. Kiss me, fuck me, hurt me... I won't say no to anything tonight, Sir."

I pondered her words, wondering whether I should give in. A long night stretched ahead of me, promising hours of solitude I would surely spend thinking about Lyra and what could have been. The thoughts about finding a perfect submissive would fill my subconscious yet again. I'd be wondering about whether a woman who could satisfy me even existed long into the night.

The girl misconstrued my silence as denial, and her bottom lip wobbled as she moved in closer, never quite touching me. Our eyes locked and she leaned in to whisper in my ear.

"I'll do anything you want, Sir... You can fuck all my holes. My pussy, my ass, my mouth—they're all yours, all for you... Please?"

"Fine," I said firmly, moving back and motioning for her to follow me to the lift that would take us directly to my penthouse. "Come on then. I'm not waiting up for you."

Finding my perfect woman would have to wait a while longer. I'd already made up my mind—that night was going to be all about pleasure.

My pleasure.

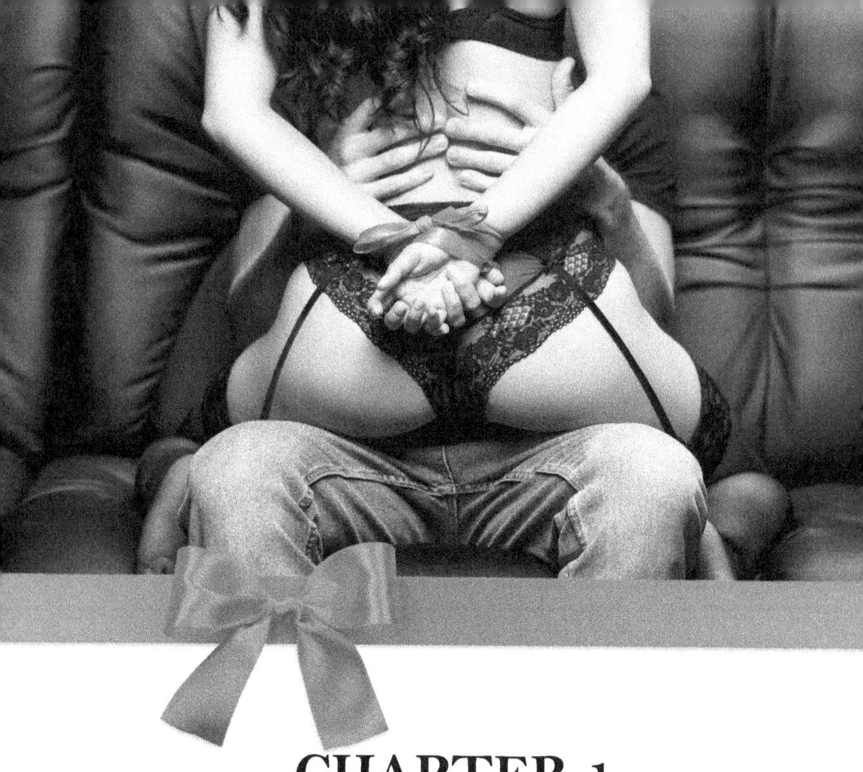

CHAPTER 1

Amicia

"*It's just not good enough.*"

The words echoed in my mind as I made my way down the wintry street. *Not good enough, for how many times in a row?* At times it felt like I'd never make it. And normally, I managed to lift my head higher and make the best of it. But that day—*just that day*—I was letting it get to me.

Every single time, the same answer. Every week, another rejection. It didn't matter where I went. Nobody was going to give me a job as a dancer without me having done any dance training. And I couldn't *afford* training.

At twenty-two, I was nearing the wrong end of my prime shot. I wanted to be a dancer. I'd dreamed of it my entire life, but my foster parents never had any money to pay for traditional lessons. I learned by myself, watching videos, reading books. I danced to music the way I wanted to. But to succeed in the highly competitive world of cutthroat ballerinas, I didn't have the education I should've started building early on. I brought raw passion to an artform that required precision and years of training.

I needed to do this. Especially now that Margaret was gone.

Currently, there was only one job that was hiring dancers like me, and while it wasn't the classiest place to work at, it paid well, and at least I got to do what I loved.

I pushed the door of *Le Cabaret* open, sliding into the room unnoticed. They *never* noticed me. Not until I started dancing. When I twirled, every pair of eyes in the room followed me.

As I entered, a figure bumped into me from behind, making me stumble forward and crash to the floor. Before I managed to get a look at him, I'd caught the attention of my least favorite person in the place.

"Amicia, get the hell up." Two bouncers stood by the front door, all broad shoulders and overstretched muscle. One of them, Skull, was calling me over. He had a neck tattoo of his namesake reaching from his chest to his chin, his neck covered in tinted ink. It only made him look more frightening. All the girls were terrified of him.

I approached even though my instincts were telling me to run. But you didn't say no to Skull. He was known for roughing up girls in the back when the boss wasn't looking. And I wasn't trying to get myself hurt.

"Yes?" I asked as I came near enough. "Can I help you?"

"Yeah." Skull beamed at me, the disco light on the ceiling reflecting from his shaved head. "My friend's new here, and he wants to see some tits. I told him, Amicia's got the best pair in the damn house. And he didn't fuckin' believe it. So, you gotta settle a bet between us, darlin'. Shirt *up*."

I stared at his friend, a good-looking, brooding guy in his twenties. He smirked at me, not bothering to tell Skull to stop it. These guys were all the same. Testosterone filled monsters who thought they got *Le Cabaret* and the boss by the balls because they were tougher than us.

Everyone knew Skull was a bully. I was the only one smart, or perhaps *stupid* enough, to stand up to him.

"I don't want to," I said, trying to stay level-headed. "I have to get ready for my shift. He can see them once I'm up there."

I tried to make my way past him, and for a second, I thought I'd get away with it. But then Skull's meaty palm wrapped around my forearm, and he yanked me back.

"Did I say you had a *choice*, darlin'?" he grunted in my face, making me tremble with unwanted concern. "You never did know how to listen. I'll just do it myself, then."

He motioned his friend over, and the prick grabbed my throat, holding me firmly in place against the wall. I struggled against his firm grip, but to no avail. He easily overpowered me while Skull grabbed my coat and ripped it open. Buttons flew everywhere as I cursed out loud. It was my last good coat, Margaret's hand-me-down, and I couldn't afford a new one, not if I wanted to pay for training.

Skull wasn't done yet. He pried my hands away from my body, forcing me to lean my ass against them and cage them behind me. Then, he lifted my sweater. Because I was working, I hadn't worn underwear, not wanting to leave behind a bra or panty line. Of course, now it wasn't helping matters much—Skull got easy access to my breasts, leering at my body as he and his friend held me in place.

"Look at her," he muttered. "She got those ghost nipples. Almost in-fucking-visible, same color as the rest of her. Makes your mouth water, don't it?"

The newly hired bouncer nodded. They were salivating over me. "Will you let me go, please? I need to get ready for my shift."

"No, I don't think we will," Skull grumbled. "I'm not done with you just yet, darlin'. See, this is the best part." He turned toward his buddy now, chuckling as he reached for me, his clammy fingers cold against my skin. "You pinch 'em, and they turn purple. Fuckin' *purple*. Not even red. See?"

He pinched my nipple so hard I cried out in pain. My eyes shot daggers at him as I hissed, "That's because you're bruising them, you piece of *shit*."

"Now now, watch your tongue," Skull reminded me, coming up close and glaring at me. His spittle flew from his lips and landed on my cheek. I recoiled in disgust, which only made him loathe me more. "You don't want to get it cut out some day."

"Jeez, Skull," I said, unable to stop myself. "I wonder which one of the girls turned you down today to put you in such a foul mood."

He scowled at me, then nodded at his friend and they both let go of me. "I'm takin' your tips tonight, darlin'. You got your tongue to thank for that."

"No, please." How quickly I was reduced to begging… *Damn Skull.* "I really need that money, Skull. Please."

He just laughed in my face, not even bothering with a response as he pulled his new friend back to guard the door. *Shit.* I kept walking to the dressing rooms, cursing inwardly for fucking up so badly. Even less money, and I was already barely making rent.

I arrived in the dressing room to the usual flutter of activity. Women in various stages of undress were flitting about the room, wearing jeweled lingerie, feather boas and *always* high heels with stockings. I slid onto my usual seat between my two friends, Evangeline and Rosabella. Evangeline winced when she saw the state of my coat.

"Got greeted by Skull and his new friend, did you?" she asked as she powdered her nose.

"More like ambushed." I groaned, taking my coat off and putting it under the long vanity table that ran the length of the room. "God, he's getting worse every day. We're going to have to organize a coup."

"Don't I know it," Rosabella spoke up from beside me, lifting her turtleneck and showing me a set of fingerprint bruises.

I winced. "They got you as well?"

"Last night after my shift," she sighed, spraying perfume on her jet-black hair. "You're right, Amicia. We need to start fighting back." She got up, smoothing out her barely-there burlesque-themed outfit. "Alright ladies. Wish me luck."

"Good luck," Evangeline and I said in unison.

With a sigh, I fixed my gaze on my reflection in the lit-up mirror. My long dark hair was lustrous in the light. I added curlers to it as Evangeline told me a story from her other workplace. She worked at a café to make ends meet, and she was also going to school. *Good on her.* She'd get out of *Le Cabaret* sooner than the rest of us.

I applied thick false lashes, making my blue eyes stand out. My olive-toned complexion started to glow as I put on a shimmering bronzing powder, and my hair came down in luxurious waves.

Evangeline and I picked each other's outfits. For her, a red feather boa to go with the scarlet leatherette basque and silky black thong. For me, an ensemble in light pink—suspenders, garter belt, a bra with lace and sequins, and a pearl-trimmed pink thong. We both put on stockings and heels to complete the look.

We were dancing half an hour apart, and I waved Evangeline off as she made her way onto the stage to the sound of catcalls and dirty words being tossed around the room.

I waited in the backstage where there was always a flurry of activity. The other girls were getting ready, shooting me friendly smiles or jealous glances depending on how much they liked me. There was a hierarchy in *Le Cabaret*, and I'd worked hard to fight my way to the top of the food chain. I needed to keep my composure and stay cool as the other girls fought for the spots below me. The wise ones made friends with me. The foolish younger ones spewed their venom at me. Those never lasted long at *Le Cabaret*.

I waited until Evangeline finished, my eyes following her moves on the stage. She was a good dancer, but she didn't have the innate calling for it that I felt. The patrons loved her because she teased them. She'd mastered the art of prying out twenties, sometimes even fifties, out of them.

I was the only one who got hundred-pound bills. Evangeline was merely a supporting act for the Kitty—my pseudonym— show.

Minutes later, Evangeline rushed backstage with a big smile on her face, flashing me a bill for a hundred bucks. "Look what I got today! It's my first one!"

"I'm so happy for you," I gushed with her, kissing her cheek before she disappeared into the powder room, all glitter and smiles. It was my turn to make money now, though I knew Skull would end up taking it all away from me by the time the day was over. But I'd still be paid for dancing, and a couple hundred quid was better than nothing.

The music changed to a dark, moody song I'd picked myself. I moved the best to emotional music. The notes swayed through me, making my body twist in ways that got every man in that room hard. I knew what I was doing, and I was determined to get through the night without any further hiccups. My face-off with Skull and the new bouncer had been more than enough for one day.

"Kitty! Kitty! Kitty!" The patrons were beginning to chant outside, and I smiled to myself as I finally entered the stage. They whooped and yelled my name as I stood with my back to the crowd, waiting for the music to kick off to its crescendo.

Here, on the stage of Le Cabaret, I was finally the star I'd always dreamed of being.

The music kicked off, and so did I. I whirled around, my eyes covered in a pink lace mask and—hopefully—making me unrecognizable. I was wearing my signature kitten mask, made of pink sequins on that day. I made my way to the front of the catwalk and began to move.

I always structured my dancing around my outfit. Today, I was the innocent kitten in pink—mimicking licking my paws, crawling on all fours, dancing as if I were playing with a toy. They went wild before I even took my clothes off. Bills were tucked into my bra, into my panties. Smaller bills covered the catwalk. I usually left those for the younger girls. Some of them were in even worse situations than I was.

The time came for me to take my bra off, and I hesitated, shyly regarding the men before me before unclasping it in the front. Roars and demands for me to take it off followed, and through it all, my gaze searched the crowd to find someone to focus on.

Sometimes I got lucky, finding a handsome man in the crowd who looked kinder than the rest of the patrons. Sometimes I picked Charles, a regular who was seventy years old and had lost his wife a decade ago. Since then, he'd been to *Le Cabaret* every night, spending most of his pension to watch women fifty years his junior dancing on the stage.

But Charles was nowhere to be found that night.

Instead, my eyes settled on a figure in the back, shaded by the lack of lights in the VIP booth. He was wearing a clean-cut, expensive suit, with a black shirt, and a black tie. His face was in the shadows, and I squinted through my mask, trying to get a better look. There was a woman there too, which surprised me. Even from my position, I could read her body language. She was pissed he'd brought her there.

"Bra off! Bra off! Bra off!" the patrons chanted, quickly transporting me from my daydream to reality. I smiled seductively, removing my bra and dangling it from my fingertips, while my other hand timidly hovered over my breasts, hiding my bruised nipples. I'd tried to correct the damage Skull had done with loose powder, but I had a feeling the purple would still show through.

The crowd let out a collective gasp as my bra fluttered to the catwalk, and I pulled my hand back. My breasts bounced free, but I wasn't done teasing them yet—pink sequin hearts with tassels covered my nipples, making them laugh and want more. More money came, and I hated myself for wasting such a money-maker dance tonight, when Skull would steal all my earnings.

As I danced, I couldn't take my eyes off the stranger in the VIP booth. Still unable to see his face, I decided to dance for him, as if it were only the two of us in *Le Cabaret*. I twirled, my hands gliding down my curves, my eyes permanently locked on the stranger's shadowed face.

I removed my thong next, and this time, there was no room to be shy. My pussy was exposed, shaved save for a little line of dark hair leading down to my center. I touched myself, innocent strokes of my fingers as the men cheered me on. When I rubbed my pussy, my fingers came away wet. The fantasy of the mysterious man in the VIP area had turned me on.

Soon, my dance came to end, and I made my way off the stage to the sound of the patrons demanding more. I wouldn't want to be the girl going on after me. They all wanted more Kitty.

In the backroom, I quickly changed out of my clothes and removed my makeup. Evangeline and Rosabella were both gone, and they were my best friends in the joint. I did get along with some of the other girls, but we weren't exactly close.

I was ready to leave in twenty minutes, grabbing my things and heading out through the back exit, doing my best to avoid the bouncers. I hadn't seen Skull since I came in, which was a good thing. The day's earnings felt like a heavy burden in my bag, which I held onto for dear life, my fingers frozen from the chilly London night.

"What's the rush, darlin'?"

Fuck. I turned around in the street, which was deserted. This wasn't the best part of town during the day, let alone in the nighttime when I usually made my way back to my apartment. I'd worked hard to afford a place in a slightly less dangerous district, but my walks home were always filled with nervousness and anxiety. It wouldn't be the first time I'd gotten cornered—either by Skull or one of the other bouncers, or even a patron from *Le Cabaret.*

"Just trying to get home," I muttered as Skull caught up with me, standing in front of me and walking backward with a shit-eating grin on his face.

"Think you're forgetting somethin'," he said, spitting on the concrete before coming to a stop on the pavement. I bumped against him, groaning when he grabbed me by the hair and tossed me to the other side of the street as if I weighed nothing.

"Please, Skull," I managed, the air knocked right out of me. "I'll give you the money, just let me go home in peace."

"Oh yeah?" he snarled. "Is that why you were tryin' to get

home without coming to me first, bitch?"

"I wasn't," I lied through gritted teeth. "I just didn't see you inside…"

"Bullshit." He slammed me back, and I stumbled backward as he descended on me. "I don't fuckin' like it when my bitches lie to me. So now, you're gonna pay for it."

CHAPTER 2

Grayson

"Please don't do this, Sir." Lyra was a mess, makeup running down her face, black streaks of mascara lining her cheeks. "Please, I want to stay with you, I want to be yours, don't let me go…"

The car slowed to a stop. A huge country house loomed before us, magnificent in the late winter day. I turned to face Lyra. Unbeknownst to her, this wasn't easy for me either. But she'd served her purpose. I'd kept her for long enough. Now, I was done. It was time for a new plaything.

"I'm sorry, Lyra," I told her, handing the beautiful red-haired vixen an envelope with her cash, and the photos I'd taken of her. "It's time now. You have to go."

"Please, Sir," she murmured. "Don't let me go, I don't want the money, I just want you."

"Unfortunately, I don't want you." My voice was calm and collected. I motioned for Kai to get her out of the car, and he opened the door, prying her off the backseat while she kicked and punched him, desperately trying to stay with me.

It was always like this when I let them go. They *all* wanted to stay with me. The problem was, none of them kept my attention for longer than a few weeks. I was a spoiled man. I got bored easily.

Lyra began to howl as Kai removed her from the car. The door closed; the sound of her wailing blocked out. I stretched my legs, smoothing down my suit. And so, the hunt for a new toy was beginning.

I watched Kai deposit Lyra in front of her parents' house with mild interest. It would take her a few months to get over me, sure, but after that, she'd be better off. When I had met her, she hadn't even known she was kinky. I'd always have fond memories of extracting her first *'Yes, Sir'* from those full, bee-stung lips.

But now, as she stumbled toward the house and Kai returned to the car, I was restless and bored. I wanted a new plaything, and I wanted her then and there.

Once my right-hand-man was next to me, the driver pulled away, leaving Lyra in front of her parents' home. Kai seemed to sense my mood and left me in peace until we were almost at the penthouse.

"Sir, if I may," he spoke up then. "Another auction will be happening soon at Couture House. I could get you a list of the girls. Perhaps you will find someone to your liking."

"Another auction?" I repeated thoughtfully. "Get me the list,

I'll look it over. But tonight, I want to have some fun."

"Certainly, Sir. May I suggest sending someone up to the penthouse? Perhaps the Sullivan twins tonight?"

"No." My answer was firm. I got out of the car, waiting for the bellboy to run outside and hold an umbrella over my head as I made my way toward the building. Kai was right beside me as I pondered what to do. I was jaded and impatient, and I wanted to do something I'd remember for a long time to come. "How about a burlesque club?"

"Of course, Sir," Kai replied without missing a beat. "I'll find one you haven't been at before."

"Perfect."

I was escorted to the lift, then took the elevator with Kai who was scrolling through his phone. We arrived at my penthouse. It was a modern, elegant bachelor pad that hadn't seen the touch of a woman—*yet*. My urge to find a more permanent solution to my relationship problem had only intensified in the past year.

As I took off my coat and placed it in the walk-in wardrobe, Kai walked up behind me with his eyes lit up. "I may have found something, Sir. It's called *Le Cabaret* and it's on Berwick Street in Soho."

"Get me the VIP booth," I told him firmly as I regarded my reflection in the mirror.

My face stared back at me from the mirror. I looked younger than my thirty-eight years, but the silver hairs in my inky black hairstyle didn't lie. I worked hard on my body, long hours exercising making me lean and muscular. The shadow of stubble was ever-present on my chiseled jaw.

I was going to turn thirty-nine soon. *Too old for this.*

"And make sure I won't be bothered. By anyone."

"Of course, Sir. Are you taking a guard with you?"

I contemplated his words before shaking my head. "No, not

tonight, Kai. But I want a woman with me. Find me a date?"

"Of course, Sir."

He withdrew from the room. I knew my answer hadn't pleased him—Kai was always irrationally worried someone would realize who I was and try to force some cash out of me. But I was more worried about putting out shady business partners than some random junkie in Soho's back alley. Besides, I could defend myself perfectly well. *I'd only been made into a fool once.* At the thought, my hands formed fists at my sides.

I couldn't think about *that* failure now. I had a night at the burlesque show to get ready for. And I had a good feeling about *Le Cabaret.*

***

My date for the night was a gorgeous twenty-something socialite by the name of Addison Meyer.

She was a stunning chocolate-haired and green-eyed beauty I wanted to fucking devour, but I knew she was not kinky within ten minutes of our first conversation. I cursed inwardly as I led her to the car. She wouldn't like where our first date was happening one bit. Usually, it would have made me excited to push a woman's limits, but this one was barely a woman. She was still a girl—an innocent, darling girl who would make someone very happy one day, but that man would not be me.

As Addison chatted about her heiress lifestyle, I stared out of the window, already bored. She seemed to sense my mood and shut up. She'd seemed thrilled to be out with me at first. I supposed being pranced around town with London's most eligible, dangerous bachelor was quite the feat. But as we pulled up in front of *Le Cabaret,* her eyes widened, and I could tell our destination was not a pleasurable surprise.

"Is this where we're going?"

"Yes." I left no room for her arguments, gallantly escorting her out of the car and into *Le Cabaret*. It wasn't the classiest of establishments, but I had a feeling Kai had sent me there for a reason.

We walked inside with our arms linked, and Addison visibly recoiled when we sat down in the VIP booth. She wore a look of disapproval as we settled down and I ordered us their finest bottle of champagne. I saw the bartender wipe the thing down before they brought it over in an ice bucket, probably to remove the dust it had been gathering in their bar for years.

A staff member popped the champagne for us, and a waitress scantily clad in a thong and nipple tassels poured me a glass to sample. I nodded my approval though the drink wasn't up to my standards. But I had a feeling I wouldn't get anything better. This place was a dump.

While Addison stewed in her own fury, I watched the woman moving on the stage before us. Her tits were out, pretty pink rosebuds enticing the patrons of *Le Cabaret* to stuff their money into her thong. I wasn't impressed. Yes, the girl was pretty, but I wanted something more. I wanted someone that would take my breath away. And I wasn't sure whether *Le Cabaret* could offer someone like that. It was subpar for the time being. I wasn't easily impressed.

The music changed and the woman left the stage while the crowd demanded more. I shifted my attention to Addison, who was busy scrolling through the many notifications on her phone. She didn't even glance up, probably texting a friend to complain what a pervert Grayson Kline turned out to be. Not that I cared. She was better off with someone else, and at least we wouldn't end the night with her having a hopeless crush on me. I never encouraged those. They irritated me to no end.

Once again, the music changed, and this time the patrons started chanting along with the melody. I could make out one word—Kitty. *Was she the next dancer?* With my gaze fixed on the stage, I waited for this girl, obviously the most popular one, to come out. She had the prime slot for dancing, and the bastards in the room were eager to stuff their money down her thong. I hoped she'd be a worthy distraction. Otherwise, I'd end up very cross with Kai for sending me to this hole.

The girl walked out, a vision in pink. Everything was rosy, from her lingerie to the stockings and heels, and the cat mask that covered her face. It was made of sequins, covering the upper half of her face, with kitten ears on top, in pastel pink.

She was enchanting from the start, with her dark brown hair and the way her body swayed to the music. She looked like a timid little kitten—exactly the look her outfit demanded of her. I was engrossed in her performance, watching her move effortlessly. *A natural dancer.* You didn't see a lot of those in joints like *Le Cabaret.*

"Are you going to stare at her all night?" Addison piped up from behind me.

"More than likely, yes." I took a sip of champagne, never taking my eyes off the dancer.

"Well, then it seems like you don't need me. I might as well leave."

Prissy little bitch. "Be my guest, Addison. But be careful, those bouncers don't look like they'll be particularly nice to any woman, let alone a rich bitch who turns her nose up at them."

She huffed and puffed behind me, knowing I was right. She'd have to wait for me to escort her home, and she didn't like it one bit. I wasn't done yet, though. My eyes were glued to the stage. I was determined to watch the kitten's impressive performance to the very end, Addison be damned.

While my date was glued to her phone, I watched Kitty on the stage. She was a wonder. She was the kind of woman you'd move mountains for. My hands formed fists as I thought of having that sinful little body in them. I wanted to claim her. Hurt her. *Own her.*

She danced with ease, smooth moves making her ethereal, like an angel descended on earth. I could have fallen in love with the woman purely from the way she moved. But I stopped myself before that could happen. I'd practiced controlling myself for a long time, and I needed to know more about the mystery woman before I allowed my feelings to take over.

During her performance, Kitty saw me in the VIP booth. I wasn't certain how much she could see—we were sitting a little way off, and the lights were dimmed. But she zeroed in on me, and for the rest of her show, I felt like she was dancing only for me. My cock was painfully hard in my slacks, straining against the fabric of my trousers, eager to be inside her.

Kitty's dance took all of twenty minutes, and they went by in a blur. She was done too soon, retreating backstage and blowing kisses to her adoring audience.

I needed more.

I stood up, Addison scrambling to her feet behind me and murmuring, "Finally."

I smirked at her, saying, "Are you always this absent on your dates? I pity the next guy if you're going to spend the night glued to your phone."

Her expression darkened and she shrugged nonchalantly. "Seemed like you were distracted, so I caught up on some texts." Her eyes flashed with anger as she motioned toward the stage. "You're obviously more interested in that... *stripper*, than you ever were in me."

"You're right," I told her decidedly. "Come on, we're

leaving."

She followed me out of the *Le Cabaret*, to the front of the street where my limo was waiting. I opened the door for her, and she got in, still hopeful that something would happen between us as she gave me a suggestive look up the slit of her glittery designer dress.

"Have a safe trip home," I told her, tapping the roof of the car.

"Wait!" Addison cried out; her eyes desperate as they met mine. "Don't you want to…"

"Don't I want to *what*?"

"Well…" she bit her lower lip, making my cock jump to attention. "Maybe we could see each other again?"

Oh, this poor, naïve girl.

"I don't think so, pet," I told her with a harsh smile. "I would destroy you, and you'd never forgive me." Her eyes sparkled in the dark. "My advice? Settle down with a nice banker your parents approve of. You'll be happier that way than with me."

"But—"

I cut her protest short by closing the passenger door. I gestured for the driver to take off, and the car pulled away, leaving me alone in the street. I wasn't done just yet though. I wanted to see what Kitty looked like when she wasn't swaying on the stage.

I waited, hidden in the shadows behind *Le Cabaret*, where the dancers' entrance was located. She was bound to appear sooner or later. I couldn't wait to see her up close, but I was wary of showing my face just yet.

It took twenty minutes for a figure to appear in the back alley, and I slid deeper in the shadows as she made her way down the dark street. I knitted my brows together. *She shouldn't have been walking around alone like that.* This wasn't the best part of town, after all.

I watched her closely, remaining hidden in the dark. She was medium height, with an impossibly slender waist and a perfect hourglass figure. Her face, though hidden by a knitted hat, was devoid of makeup and perfect in its natural state. Her coat didn't have any buttons, so she clutched it closed around her slender body. She had an olive-toned complexion, with sparkling blue eyes and perfect white teeth. Kitty was a natural beauty, and I knew what lay beneath her clothes was just as perfect.

The temptation to leave my hiding spot was strong, but I resisted. And just as well, because a burly, broad-shouldered figure followed my girl into the back alley, his hands tucked into the pockets of his puffer jacket.

"What's the rush, darlin'?" he snarled at her, and I growled out loud when he grabbed her. The bastard was stronger and bigger than she was. She didn't have a chance in hell of fighting him off, and I hated the piece of shit for using his strength against her.

I observed their conversation which was quickly turning into the guy intimidating Kitty until she pulled back from him in fear. *I had to intervene.* Precautions be damned. This bastard was going to hurt her, and I couldn't just stand back and watch it happen.

But I didn't have a choice. I couldn't allow Kitty to see me just yet. I needed to bide my time. I watched the guy bully her until she handed him a thick wad of cash—probably her earnings from the night.

My fists clenched as I watched her retreat, like prey trying to escape its predator. She used the opportunity when the guy was counting her cash to run down the street and disappear into one of the side alleys. The man, obviously pleased with his accomplishments, pocketed the money, and made his way back to the building. But I was waiting for him, and I was going to make him pay.

I cornered the guy, stepping ahead of him and caging him

between the wall and my broad shoulders.

"Going somewhere?" I asked him calmly.

"Get out of my way," the guy snarled before taking a good look at me, his mind probably still on the cash he'd just stolen. "Who the hell do you think you are?" He raised his eyes to meet mine, and a look of fear crossed his face. "Oh, Mr. Kline, I'm sorry, I didn't know it was you…"

"Who was the girl?" I motioned down the street Kitty had disappeared down. "Why'd you take her money?"

"Just one of the dancers," the guy shrugged. He had an ugly skull in flames tattooed on his throat. "I took what belongs to me, is all."

"How does it belong to you if she earned it?" I demanded, and he narrowed his eyes at me.

"I don't want any problems, Mr. Kline."

"Then do as you're told," I said coolly. "Are you willing to return the money to its rightful owner and apologize *profusely* for taking it in the first place?"

The beast in front of me gnashed its teeth together. He didn't like this one bit, but he also knew how much power I held. I could have his balls crushed with the click of my fingers, and he'd be powerless against me.

"Just think of how badly I can hurt you," I told him firmly. "Then think how easy it would be to just start being a decent human being and returning what you stole. And if you do, you have better odds of me letting you live through this."

His eyes widened. "I didn't mean nothin' bad, I just needed some cash, Sir…"

"I don't care." I backed away, putting a pair of gloves on my hands. I was done dirtying them with scum like this bouncer. He was obviously from the wrong side of the tracks since he knew me by name. "You'll return the money tomorrow. And you'll apologize to Kitty. If I find out you haven't, I'll make sure your tattoo becomes a real thing. I'd quite enjoy seeing your skull go up in flames, I think."

"Please, Sir…" The guy was backtracking, holding his hands up to defend himself. "I'll give you the money now, just leave me alone."

"No." I scowled at him. "I want a sincere apology out of you. Tomorrow, by midnight at the latest. Got it?"

He nodded reluctantly, scratching the back of his bald head. "Sorry, Sir. Didn't know Kitty was one of yours."

I smiled, muttering, "Not yet she isn't. But she will be. She just doesn't know it yet."

CHAPTER 3

Amicia

The next day, Skull was nowhere to be seen. I was relieved to find *Le Cabaret* safe from its most evil bully—it was a welcome reprieve in my daily routine.

Evangeline was out for the day, working her other job, but Rosabella was there, dancing hours before me, so we just exchanged a quick hug at the door before she left.

On days when my two friends weren't working, I felt lonely. I got along with the other girls, but there was always the underlying feeling of jealousy between us, which I didn't like one bit.

A younger girl, Capri, was there though, and I'd gotten along with her in the past, so I set up my makeup station next to hers, greeting her with a warm smile.

Capri had only been with us for a few weeks, but she'd already gotten a steady following of patrons from the club. They loved her sweet innocence, that porcelain skin and her dark locks—a sharp contrast, like ivory and ebony.

"You look anxious today," I said as she dropped her powder brush for the third time. "Everything okay?" I worried it was something to do with Skull, but since he was gone for the day, I figured it had to be something else.

"I'm just…" she sighed, picking up the brush and applying cherry blusher to her sharp cheeks. "Nervous about something I have coming up."

"Oh?" I raised my brows, curling my hair with a flat iron until it shone in the light. "Anything I can help with?"

"I don't think so," she laughed anxiously. "Unless…" She eyed me with a curious look. "I suppose I could tell you…"

"Tell me what?"

"I'm doing something to make some extra money." She glanced around the room before sliding closer to me with her chair. "Don't tell the other girls."

"Oh, Capri." I squeezed her knee. "Please don't tell me it's what I think it is… It's never a good idea, especially here, with Skull waiting for the first chance to jump down your throat and steal your money."

"It's not here," Capri spoke up warily. "It's with a reputable agency. They're called Couture House. Have you heard of them before?"

"Couture House?" I tried the name out on my lips, shaking my head. "No, I don't think I have. What do they do?"

"They run auctions," Capri whispered.

"For?"

"For…" Her eyes sparkled. "For women, and the services we can provide."

"Oh Capri, I don't know if that's a good idea…"

"It's a lot of money," she went on defensively. "I get ten percent of the profits."

"Only ten percent?"

"It's a lot," she said. "To *me*, it's a lot."

"I know." I squeezed her hand for reassurance. "I'm just worried about this being the right thing to do. You're so young, Capri… Didn't you just turn eighteen?"

She nodded, tight lipped as I waited for her answer. "I'm old enough."

"And what are you auctioning off?"

She leaned forward to whisper in my ear, and my eyes widened. "Capri!"

"What?" she asked. "I've held onto it for long enough. This way, at least I'll make some money."

My instincts were kicking in. I wanted to make sure she'd be okay, wanted to come with her if only to ensure no one took advantage. "Maybe I should come with you."

"That would be great," she gushed. "What will you auction?"

"No, not like that," I muttered.

"But Amicia, you could make some money," she said. "*Lots.*"

"How much?" I asked, not expecting her whispered answer one bit.

"Well, if I sell mine for one million… which they said was the going price… I'll get a hundred thousand."

"What?" I nearly choked. "That's… *life-changing* money."

"I know," she nodded eagerly. "You could auction a night with yourself. It could go for five-hundred thousand, and you'd get fifty out of it."

Those numbers were staggering and remarkable, making me

bite my lower lip as I considered her words. *I could do it.* It would mean finally being able to pay for dancing lessons. It would mean crawling out of the hole Margaret had dug for me. My life would change.

"Who do I need to contact?" I asked Capri, my voice a low whisper.

She smiled, digging in her pink backpack, and pulling out a business card. "Here. His name is Dmitri Sokolov. He'll tell you everything you need to do."

"Thank you." I pocketed the card with a guilty expression. I shouldn't have been as excited as I was about this. It meant going against everything I stood for, going back on my own promise to never sell myself. But what choice did I have? I was twenty-two years old, with staggering debt left over from Margaret's death and dance lessons I desperately needed but could never afford.

I danced in a blur that night, my thoughts preoccupied with the business card stuck in the pocket of my jacket. I wasn't sure whether I'd call Dmitri Sokolov, but a little nagging voice at the back of my mind insisted I should give it a go.

***

The next day, the thought of Couture House was still front and center in my mind, but so was the guilt I felt every time I thought of the opportunity Capri had offered me.

Nasty little thing, Margaret's voice echoed in my head. *Nothing but a cheap slut. I knew you'd end up like this. Like the whore you are.*

But the bright side was, I had another audition that day, for a production of Romeo and Juliet that I was extremely excited about. I had spent hours getting ready for it after work, staying up late until I was convinced I had the moves down pat. I learned from a video I'd found online and could only hope it would be enough to convince the casting director I was the right fit for the role.

As I made my way to the theater where the auditions were being held, Dmitri Sokolov' business card burned a hole in my pocket. I was painfully aware of it the whole time, even as I got changed into my leotard and a pair of worn-out ballet slippers I'd bought at a consignment store.

I stayed in the waiting room with the other girls vying for the role. It was always nerve-wracking to see my competition. These girls weren't just stunning, with expensive clothes and hairstyles, they also had the training I lacked.

A woman with round-shaped glasses called our names off a list one by one, and the girls disappeared into the room. Some of them came out elated, others looked down, some were even crying. But it was always like this at dancing auditions. It was a cutthroat world in this industry, and it wasn't an uncommon sight to see the prospects in tears. I'd been told I needed to lose weight, change my hair color, or that I was hopelessly plain plenty of times before. It all came with the job.

I wasn't called for ages, making me think they'd forgotten about me. By the end, only two of us remained—a pretty blonde with sparkling grey eyes, and me.

As we were sitting in the waiting area, a group of people exited the audition room, and the woman who'd been calling us in told us they were taking a short break and would be back in twenty. We nodded, exchanging shy glances as the group left the room.

"Just my luck," I muttered. "Being called last when I have somewhere to be."

"Likewise," the blonde smiled at me. "I'm already late for my dance lesson. You too?"

I tried to hide the shame burning my cheeks, giving her a non-committal nod. "Is this your first audition?"

She nodded with a nervous smile. "That obvious, huh?"

"It's the nerves," I laughed. "But trust me, those never go away, not even after years of doing this. You just get better at hiding them."

We chatted easily, but both of us went quiet the moment the casting team walked back into the room. One of them, a tall man with blond hair, stopped and stared at me.

"You look familiar," he muttered. "Do I know you?"

I looked up at him and a feeling of dread settled in the pit of my stomach. *Fuck.* He was one of the regulars at *Le Cabaret.* I could only pray he wouldn't recognize me.

"No, I don't think so," I chirped.

"Strange," he muttered. "I rarely forget a face." He gave me an appreciative one-over before adding, "Especially one like yours."

I flushed, looking away to hide my embarrassment. He kept staring at me until the group went into the theater, and he followed behind them.

In minutes, the woman who'd been calling out names reappeared.

"Kensington Waverly," she called out, and the blonde stood up.

"Oh God." She swallowed, pale with nervousness.

"You'll be okay," I smiled at her. "Good luck."

"Thanks," she whispered before disappearing into the room. Her audition took the longest. By the time the door opened again, I was an impatient mess, eager to get the casting call over with. I had a shift at *Le Cabaret* that night again, and I couldn't miss it. Maybe this time, Skull wouldn't take my money away from me.

I had twenty minutes left before I absolutely had to leave

to make it to my shift on time before she reappeared, her face a blotchy red mess.

"Is everything okay?" I asked, furrowing my brows at the sight of her.

"No, it's not!" she cried out.

"Amicia Romano," the woman called out. "Come on, no dillydallying, we don't have all day."

I flushed. They didn't care about my time, but their own was precious enough to rush me along.

I walked into the casting room where the casting committee was waiting. I greeted them, but no reply came from the group. There were two men and a woman there, and they all regarded me with bored looks. They were probably exhausted from their long day. I knew I wouldn't impress them with my looks alone. Luckily for me, my dancing was the star of the show, and I just *knew* I was right for the role.

"Get into position," the gray-haired woman sitting behind the long table mumbled, sounding bored. "Start the music."

The woman who'd called me in sat down at the piano, stretching her fingers and starting to play. The familiar notes of Profokiev's melody awoke something deep within me, and I got into the starting position, ready to impress.

As the melody changed to Juliet's soliloquy, I began to dance. I twirled and twisted my body in tune with the music, managing to forget all about the people watching me as I made the dance my own.

I felt their eyes on me as I moved through the room. The man from *Le Cabaret* was making me nervous, but I tried not to let it show. *Confidence, even when faked, could hide a multitude of sins.*

I danced until I was out of breath, and the piano player slowed to a stop. I stopped in the fourth position and was shocked to hear two of the casting members clapping for me.

I looked up with a bright smile, my eyes fixing on the other man in the team, with a head of thick silver hair.

"That was…" The man's eyes sparkled. "Unforgettable. You were absolutely fantastic. Magnificent."

"Thank you," I managed, fighting off the traitorous blush in my cheeks as I looked down, tucking a stray strand of hair behind my ear. "I'm so glad you enjoyed it."

"It was breathtaking," the grey-haired woman added with a tight-lipped smile. "I'm impressed. We certainly saved the best for last."

I smiled before shifting my attention to the third man in the group, the one I was most nervous about, since he was the one who could possibly recognize me from *Le Cabaret*. He tapped his finger against his chin as he regarded me with a naughty look. *Oh God. Had he recognized me?*

"It was good," he finally said, never taking his eyes off me. "Very good."

"Thank you," I whispered.

"We'll be in touch," he ended the conversation. "Expect a call soon."

"Thank you so much." I was giddy with excitement as I shook their hands and made my way out of the room. I expected to see Kensington there, but she was gone. I gathered my things before making my way out of the theater's back exit. If I hurried along, I'd make it to *Le Cabaret* just in time for my shift.

"Wait up!" a voice called out from behind me as I made my way out the back alley. I turned around, coming face-to-face with the member of the casting team who'd told me I looked familiar. "Amicia. Wait."

I stopped, turning around. "Yes?"

He reached me in a few quick steps, grinning widely. "I

remember where I know you from."

I paled. *Fuck*. He *had* recognized me.

"Oh?" I asked lamely.

"Don't play dumb," he said with a leering smile, taking a long look at me and prompting me to hold my coat around my body tighter. "I'd recognize those twists and turns anywhere, *Kitty*."

"Please... I..." I stuttered, and he laughed at me.

"Everyone in there was impressed with you," he went on. "However, as I'm sure you understand, we cannot allow a... *stripper*... to dance the lead role in our production."

"I..." I swallowed. "Of course, I understand."

"Unless of course..." He put out the bait, and then shook his hand dismissively. "No, I don't think you'd like my suggestion."

"Suggestion?" I repeated, giving him a questioning look. "What suggestion?"

"Well," he went on with a smirk. "I did always like your moves, Kitty."

I knew where this was going. As much as I wanted to stop the bastard in his tracks, I wanted him to finish, hoping for the slight chance that he wouldn't be the prick I'd expected him to be.

"What do you mean?" I questioned him, raising my brows.

"What I mean," he went on, taking a step forward and taking my hand in his. "I can keep your little secret if you show me some more of that dancing you love to do so much, when you take your clothes off. In *private*."

My blood boiled at the thought. This was blackmail, pure and simple. The others would have given me the starring role, but this bastard was intent on making me grovel for it.

"I don't think so," I hissed, snatching my hand away from him. "And I don't appreciate your lewd proposition."

"Lewd?" He laughed, his demeanor changing in a split second. "You're one to talk, Amicia. But alright. Consider it a missed opportunity." He smirked. "I was going to put out a good word for you with the other productions. But now… Don't be surprised if you don't get a role for a long fucking time. *Kitty*."

The man was vile, and I wasn't going to stick around to listen to more of his insults. I ran down the alleyway. Thankfully, he didn't follow me.

I was going to be late for my shift, but I found it hard to care. Tears burned my eyes as I walked the six blocks from the audition to *Le Cabaret*. I felt ashamed. Taken advantage of. And I knew the man had been right. There would be no more roles for me, not with his word against mine.

I remembered the card Capri had given me, the weight of it heavy in my pocket.

With trembling fingers, I took the card out, reading the name and number again. Was I brave enough to call? Brave enough to risk it?

I didn't have a choice.

I had to do it.

Pulling my cheap cell phone from my coat's pocket, I typed in the number from the business card. After taking a long breath, I hit the call button. *Here we go.*

It rang for ages before a rattly sounding voice finally picked up. "Dmitri Sokolov, how can I help you?"

"H-H-Hello," I stuttered, hating myself for coming off weak. "I… I'm not sure I'm calling the right place…"

A low chuckle put me right in my place. He knew what I was calling about, of course he did. "Hello, little doll. Are you calling me about the auction?"

"Y-Yes," I managed, raising my chin up high with determination. "I'm calling about Couture House. I'd like to participate in the auction."

"Who sent you?"

"What?"

"Your reference," he repeated. His voice was accented, but his English was perfect. "Who told you about Couture House?"

"Uh, Capri. Capri Sorrento."

"Ah, Capri," he laughed easily. "Such a wonderful, sweet little girl. And your name?"

"Amicia. Amicia Romano."

"Another Italian?"

"Yes, well…" I swallowed. "My parents were. I never knew them."

"Tragic," he said, the word devoid of emotion. "You need money?"

"I do," I went on.

"You know Capri from *Le Cabaret*?"

"Yes."

"Ah. And which one are you?" His voice was amused.

"I… My performing pseudonym is… Kitty."

"Kitty?" he repeated, sounding more and more amused. "The infamous Kitty?"

"I… suppose so, yes."

"Perfect." His voice was a low purr now. "You'll do just fine with us, Amicia. Or shall I call you Kitty? Which do you prefer?"

"Amicia is fine," I muttered. "So… what do you need from me?"

"To show up in Notting Hill, at an address that will be sent to this number, December first at six p.m. We will prepare you for the auction."

"But you don't even know what I look like," I reminded him, and he chuckled.

"Of course I do. I know everything, Amicia, as you'll soon find out. Will I see you on December first?"

"Don't you need to know what I'll be auctioning?" I

questioned.

"There's only one thing we're interested in," he said smoothly. "And I think you know what it is." I swallowed, hating him. "I only need to know one thing."

"What's that?"

"Which hole are you selling, Kitty?"

CHAPTER 4

Grayson

Kai was away for the next few weeks for me, which meant I had to deal with my third-in-command, Florian. He was Kai's younger brother, and while he was perfectly capable of running errands, he was too young to keep a level head. He often lost his cool, making him an unreliable companion. Still, he'd have to do until Kai returned.

That day, Florian's duty was to report back on Skull. I hoped for the man's sake he'd heeded my warning, but something told me he'd done anything but. As Florian returned to the penthouse, his grim expression told me everything I needed to know.

"No luck?" I asked, and he shook his head.

"I was inside *Le Cabaret*. He was still bullying the girls, demanding their money."

"Did you see my girl?" I demanded. Another shake of Florian' head.

"I think she had the day off. How would you like us to proceed, Sir?"

"We're going to face that bastard once again," I said after a moment's pause. "We'll wait until his shift is over. I want you to come with me."

"Of course, Sir."

"That'll be all." I turned my attention back to the files I was working on.

"Another thing, Sir."

"Yes?"

"Here is the list you requested." Florian handed me a manila envelope. "In there you will find photos, names and a brief bio on every one of the women being sold tonight, along with what they are auctioning off."

"Perfect. Thank you, Florian." I dismissed him with the wave of my fingers, and he left me alone with my thoughts and the envelope, staring at me from my desk.

As the door shut behind Florian, I wondered whether I should even bother looking at the list. My thoughts were still with the stunning Kitty from *Le Cabaret*. But I needed a distraction badly, so I ended up picking up the folder, filing through the photos.

The women were all breathtakingly beautiful. Of *course* they were—otherwise they'd never have gotten in. I went through file after file, flipping through one woman to another, their names all blending together. Reese. Gianna. Capri. Amicia.

The last one made me stop in my tracks. I hesitated with my hand on the page, then covered up the top part of her face to make sure. Yes, it was her. My Kitty in the flesh.

I couldn't believe my luck. How I'd been hoping for a new toy, lusting after the beautiful dancer, only to have her fall in my lap like this. *It was almost too easy.*

Now I knew without a doubt I'd have to pay a visit to the auction. It was the perfect opportunity to get what I wanted. My Kitty still had no idea who I was, and that I'd been watching her closely. *She'd be in for a nice surprise.*

But first, there was something else I needed to do.

***

Le Cabaret was even seedier in the morning light. It was past four a.m., the most popular girls at the joint were long gone, and the place was filled with questionable characters when Quentin, my driver, pulled up in front of it.

Florian and I got out of the cover, walking toward the building without exchanging a word. We'd already discussed what was going to happen. Florian may not have been as level-headed as Kai, but he was an important cog in my machine.

As soon as we walked into *Le Cabaret*, we caught the attention of one of the guards, a thirty-something man who resembled Skull, with his shaved head and garish tattoos.

"We're closed," he told Florian. There was a woman draped on his lap and another serving him drinks while he slapped her nearly bare, firm ass. But as soon as the man's eyes zeroed in on me and he realized who I was, he was off his chair, almost too eager in his efforts to make me feel welcome. "Oh, Mr. Kline… Welcome. I'm so sorry for my rudeness."

I waved my hand dismissively, my eyes scanning the place to find Skull.

"Are you looking for someone, Sir?" the bouncer asked.

"A man named Skull," I told him. "We've got some unfinished business."

"Of course. I'll find him for you."

"We'll wait for him behind the club," Florian said, and the guard nodded before disappearing into the backstage area of *Le Cabaret*. We made our way toward the back exit, and on the way, a woman draped her arm over my shoulders, giving me a seductive look.

"Care for a dance, handsome?" she purred.

"Get your hands off him," Florian hissed. "Don't you know who he is?"

The girl, a pretty young thing with a pale pink wig and dark blue eyes, smiled at me before a look of recognition crossed her face. It almost made me sad that she'd recognized me. It meant she knew too much about the corrupt, dark side of London.

"Now now, Florian," I said gently, suddenly empathetic toward the girl. She was so young. "It's alright." I gently pried her arms off me, and she gave me a sheepish look. "Why do you work here?"

"I need the cash," the girl muttered.

"What for?"

"My… my grandma," she finally managed. "She's sick. And she can't work. So it's just us."

"Are you eighteen?" I demanded, my hard gaze drilling into hers and demanding she tell me the truth. After a moment's hesitation, she shook her head no.

Anger pooled in my belly at the thought of the poor girl exposing herself like this when she wasn't even legal. I pulled out a wad of cash from my pocket, and the girl's eyes widened as I gave her the whole lot.

"For your grandma," I told her.

"Thank you, Sir…" She pocketed the money hastily, as if she

were afraid I'd change my mind. "What do you w-want me to do for it?" Her voice was shaky. I could tell she was afraid of what I'd ask of her, but I had no intention of making her work for my cash.

"Don't come back here," I told her firmly. "And forget all about me. What's your name?"

"Remington," she whispered.

"Alright, Remington," I said gently. "Go home. Don't come back. Say hello to grandma from me. And don't even think about doing something like this again." I motioned to Florian, and he handed her my business card begrudgingly. "Call me if you need anything else."

The girl's eyes were filled with tears as she looked at me. "Why are you doing this?"

"Because," I said firmly. "I've been where you are, and I wish I'd had someone to help me like I just helped you, before it was too late. Now go. Go!"

She scrambled to her feet, leaving the main room of *Le Cabaret* in a rush. Florian didn't comment though I could tell from the tension between us he was eager to say something. My look of disapproval was enough to shut him up, though.

We made our way to the back alley. Florian blended into the shadows while I stood right in the middle of it, my eyes focused on the back exit and waiting for Skull. He appeared moments later, his gaudy tattoo standing out against the stark paleness of his skin. When he saw me, his eyes darkened, and his hands formed fists at his sides. The stupid bastard was gearing up for a fight. *How foolish.*

"I hear you haven't done what I asked of you," I hissed at him.

"Why would I listen to you?" Skull grunted. "You have no authority. This is my corner."

"This is *London*," I told him. "*My* city. You do as I say, or you pay the price."

"What price?" he laughed at me. "I can take you, pretty boy."

"We'll see about that. Before we do, I'll give you one last shot to make things right between us. Will you return the money you stole and apologize to the girls you work with?" His response was a grunt, which made me sigh in disappointment. "I have to say, I didn't have high hopes for your intelligence when I first saw you, but you manage to disappoint me more and more every time we speak. It's your call, Skull, but trust me, you're about to regret saying no to me."

"We'll see about that," the guy snarled before lunging at me. I ducked, avoiding his punch narrowly. My hand wrapped around his neck the next second, squeezing the ugly tattoo on his throat. He never saw my other hand coming, and I hit him in the face hard enough to knock him out.

He landed on the ground with a thud. Florian pulled himself out of the shadows and approached us, while I muttered, "Search him."

Skull was a groaning mess on the ground while Florian conducted the search and showed me the contents of the bouncer's pockets. "Money, a phone, and a knife, Sir."

"How predictable," I muttered. "Give me his phone."

Florian handed me the cell, and I clicked on the camera icon before grinning at my assistant. "Pull his pants down."

"What?" Skull moaned from the ground. "What the hell are you doing?"

"Showing you your place," I replied simply before snapping a picture of his flaccid excuse for a dick. I sent off the image to his entire contact list, making sure to include his face in the shot. "Now at least the world knows you're this way because you've got a sorry excuse for a dick between your legs. Sucks to be you, don't you think?"

He snarled, but he was too weak to pick himself up. I handed Florian the phone, discarded the knife in the alley and pocketed the cash.

"You're going to pay back everything you stole," I told the bouncer. "Out of your own money. You're going to apologize to Kitty personally, and then you're going to quit this job and warn your little buddies what happens when you're a piece of shit like you. Got it?"

He glared at me, attempting to get up and lunge at me again, but Florian stepped between us, blocking the hit. *Not that I couldn't have avoided it myself.* I pushed my assistant out of the way, grabbing Skull by the shirt and muttering, "And if I ever see you near Kitty again, I'll make you wish you had never been born."

CHAPTER 5

Amicia

I didn't work that day, and I was surprised when I got the call from management asking me to show up at *Le Cabaret*. It wasn't to dance, and my paycheck wasn't due another two weeks, so I had no idea what I was getting into as I walked into the building.

The moment I sauntered in, I spotted Skull, feeling a chill go down my spine. *God, please don't let him notice me.* I couldn't handle another altercation with the brutal bouncer. He'd already shaken me up enough the last time.

But he strode right toward me, stopping me before I could make my way to the changing rooms.

"What do you want?" I hissed, trying to remain calm.

"I want to…" He shifted his weight from one foot to another. The man looked nervous, his stubble growing in on his jaw like I'd never seen it do before. He also had a bruise that had swollen his right eye shut. "I want to apologize."

"Apologize?" I stared in surprise. "For what?"

"For taking your cash," he mumbled, pushing an envelope full of bank notes toward me. "It won't happen again, you've got my word."

"What?" I gave him a critical one-over. He really was in bad shape. "What's happening here? Is this some kind of joke?"

"No," he grunted, tight-lipped as I pocketed the cash. I needed it badly, and I wasn't about to turn him down.

"Well, thanks," I muttered. "It's much appreciated, Skull."

He nodded, sidestepping, and allowing me to pass. Just as I was almost out of earshot, he called out after me. "And good on you, Amicia. For making friends in high places."

What the hell was he talking about?

***

Capri was waitressing when I walked into *Le Cabaret*. She kept sneaking glances at me. I knew as well as she did that the auction was that night. I'd already called and planned to be there, but I could still pull out at the last minute. *But would I?* First, I had a conversation with the boss I still had to sit through.

The boss of *Le Cabaret* was Pablo Capaldi, an Italian in his mid-fifties who was about as attracted to the dancers at the burlesque club as he was to a block of cheese. His boyfriend Marco lived with him in an expensive penthouse and had been leeching off him for years. Pablo himself was harmless, but Marco fed him dangerous ideas that often got the entire club in trouble.

I knocked on the door of Pablo's office, and he called me in with a cheery voice. I walked into the room which was in its usual messy state. "You wanted to see me?"

"Ah, yes, Kitty," he went on with a big grin. Another thing about Pablo—he never called us by our real names. "Come in, come in. Have a seat."

He poured himself a glass of his favorite rum while I sat down in a seat facing his desk. "How can I help you, Pablo?"

"Ah, straight to business." He grinned at me, readjusting his toupee. "I like that about you, Kitty, I like it very much." He downed his glass in one go, wincing at the burn in his throat. "I'm sure you know you're one of our most popular dancers, Kitty?"

"Your *most* popular one," I corrected him, making him chuckle.

"Indeed, indeed, my dear. So, as you can imagine, you're making us a lot of money. Lots of guests coming in to see you 'specially. Lots of them ask for you every night. But we can only let you dance four nights a week at most. Gotta keep it a little exclusive, y'know?"

I nodded uncertainly. I didn't like the overly friendly way in which he spoke. "What do you need from me, Pablo? I have somewhere to be, so get to the point, if you don't mind."

"Of course, of course." He slicked back his gelled fake hair and grinned at me again. "Well, I would like to promote you, Kitty."

"Promote me?" I raised my brows. "How?"

"Well, there is a certain, ah, shall we say—*demand*—for you, Kitty. As I said, lots of interest. Lots."

"Interest in private dances?" I interrupted. "Because I already told you, I'm not willing to do that."

"No, not quite." He gave me another one of his sleazy grins. "I want you to sleep with them."

I saw red, but I kept my cool, narrowing my eyes at the seedy character in front of me. "Excuse me, Pablo?"

"You heard me." His demeanor changed in an instant. He was no longer the friendly man who treated us like little outcast orphans. He was all business now, making it clear this wasn't a choice. "I will pick the clients. You will sleep with them and receive a percentage of the money."

"And if I decline?"

"Then today is your last day at *Le Cabaret*."

I stood up, feeling so angry I thought I would burst. Pablo didn't care though. He just stared at me with that leering smile, enjoying this rare moment of having power—over anyone but his little boy toy.

"Thank you, Pablo," I hissed.

"I trust I'll have your decision at your next shift," he smirked at me.

"No," I replied icily. "You can have it right now. Goodbye, Pablo."

I slammed the door on the way out.

***

I'd gathered my things from the changing room when Capri came rushing in, glittery and pampered from the dance she'd just performed.

"Is it true?" she gasped when she saw me standing there with a pathetic cardboard box of my things. *Being fired was the same at any job. It fucking sucked.* "Did Pablo really fire you?"

"I fired myself," I muttered, gathering the rest of my things, including my kitten masks. "I'm sorry, Capri."

"Well, it's his loss," she said, shaking her head. "Letting the best one out of all of us go… What the hell was Pablo thinking?"

I shrugged, unwilling to come up with a clever response.

"Well, it doesn't matter." She looked around to make sure nobody was listening. "You're coming tonight, aren't you?"

"Shhh, Capri." I gave her a warning look. "We shouldn't talk about that here."

"We have to," she insisted. "I'm counting on you, Amicia. Please tell me you'll be there."

I swallowed, nervously glancing around the room. I had just effectively lost my only income. I had to find another job, and fast. Before my life ended up in tatters.

"I suppose I don't have a choice," I muttered to the sound of Capri's excited squealing.

***

We met up in front of *Le Cabaret* once Capri's shift ended. It felt strange seeing the place now that I didn't work there anymore. I'd spent the rest of the evening wallowing the loss of a job I hadn't even meant to stick with.

Capri rushed out of the building in her second-hand fur coat. As always, she looked fabulous and she pulled me in for a hug, kissing my cheek as she whispered, "Are you excited?"

"Not the word I'd use," I muttered as she linked her arm with mine. "So, how reputable is this place?"

"I know a girl who's done it before. She auctioned her first time trying… you know." She winked at me, making me pale. "From behind? She got a hundred fifty grand from it."

"That's horrible," I muttered. "And perverted."

"Then why are you doing it?" Capri questioned me.

"Because I need the money."

"Don't we all."

We made our way to the auction house which was in the

Notting Hill area. The house was a historical building, and we were patted down before being allowed to enter. Once in there, our names were written down and we were ushered into a large communal shower and ordered to strip naked.

I felt humiliated, but there was nothing to be done. I had to go through with it, and it wasn't as if I hadn't been naked around other people before.

Capri and I scrubbed down before we were shown to the waxing room. The name alone made me wince, but it was nothing compared to the rough hands of the Russian women who waxed us bare, as rough as if they had a personal vendetta against us. Then, we were rubbed down with oil, our hair styled, and our makeup done.

Finally, a bored-looking man presented us with a contract each, the papers a mile long. I gave Capri a worried look, but the blonde had already scribbled her signature.

"Capri!"

"What?" She rolled her eyes. "I've already made up my mind."

I went through the pages painstakingly, obviously annoying the guy watching us until he was tapping his foot so loud, I just went to the last page, flushing as I wrote down my name on the dotted line.

"Good," he said, snatching the papers away from me. "About damn time. Now get in line. You'll be up soon."

I was too shocked to reply, and Capri and I were ushered to a line of girls waiting in the backstage. We'd been dressed in pink silk robes and nothing else, with a pair of heels on our feet. Capri looked beautiful, and from the jealous looks of the other girls, I assumed I looked good as well.

"Amicia Romano, you're up next."

My knees nearly gave out as I stood up. I tried to find Capri behind me, but it was too late. Someone shoved me from behind, and I stumbled onto the stage, shattering the first impression I'd wanted to make. Snickers and chuckling followed me as I made my way to the front of the stage, my cheeks burning brighter than any Christmas tree.

"She's twenty-two years old," the auctioneer read off his notepad, raising his brows at the lack of information on it as I took in the room before me. It was like a theater, with about sixty people watching me move on the stage. "No college degree, just a high school diploma. Well, how disappointing." He took a long, leering look at me, adding, "Though her looks almost make up for it, don't you think?"

I glared at him, but he paid it no mind, ordering me to strip on the stage. Though I'd known it was coming, my cheeks were alight with embarrassment as I pulled the belt off my silky pink robe. The crowd stared, the bright lights above me blinding as I slowly slid the robe over my shoulders.

This is what I was good at—it's why I'd wanted to be a dancer my entire life. I had the presence, the mysterious *je-ne-sais-quoi* so many others were missing. And I believed in myself passionately, despite the entire world attempting to convince me that I wasn't good enough.

It was why I was standing on that stage, after all. To be sold to the highest bidder. To receive money in exchange for my body. It would make all my dreams come true.

My body swayed to the sound of music only I could hear. Through the bright stage lights, my gaze flitted from one person in the audience to the next, trying to find a face to settle on. They were all men—older, suited-up men with unforgiving faces and hungry eyes devouring my now naked body. My hands slid down the generous curve of my waist, fingertips gliding over silky soft skin. Just then, my eyes zeroed in on a man in the third row, wearing a grey pinstripe suit with a black shirt and a black tie underneath.

His dark gaze was enough to make me stop for a single second, frozen by the weight of his stare. He was handsome in a cruel way, all sharp lines and the dark shadow of stubble that never quite went away. Dark salt-and-pepper streaked hair was slicked back, shaved closely on the sides and longer on top. He was devilishly handsome. And he screamed *danger.*

The robe fell to my feet as the audience watched, mesmerized. I danced for the man watching me and no one else. My body twisted and turned for him, my eyes glued to his as he swallowed, his Adam's apple bobbing in his throat.

He raised his paddle.

Every person's head snapped toward him.

"A hundred thousand," he said in a deep, gravelly voice.

"A hundred thousand!" the auctioneer repeated. "Do we have a higher bid?"

"Hundred fifty!" someone yelled from the crowd as I stood shivering in front of them. I was eager to cover up, my hands trembling, needing to retain some dignity. But I forced myself to keep my hands crossed at the wrists behind my back.

"Two hundred thousand." The handsome man was still staring at me, his eyes devouring my body.

"Three hundred," came the bid from a third man.

"Five hundred thousand."

The crowd gasped at the amount of money, but the stranger I'd fixated on wore a cool, unforgiving smile. He was in this to win it, and something told me he wasn't used to losing.

The bids kept coming. Finally, there were two men left bidding for me, the numbers getting closer and closer to one million dollars. I would get ten percent of that money. It was shocking how little they were willing to let me have, but to me, that amount of money was life changing.

"Seven hundred fifty thousand pounds."

The crowd wasn't even muttering anymore, they were whooping, cheering the handsome man on. The other man, an older guy in his fifties with a head of thick silver hair, grimaced and shook his head.

"Seven hundred fifty going once," the auctioneer spoke up. "Seven fifty going twice. Sold, to the highest bidder!"

My legs nearly gave out as I picked my robe off the floor. With my cheeks burning, I didn't dare look at the man who'd just spent a fortune for a single night with me. I wondered whether he knew the small amount of money I'd receive from the sale. I wondered whether he cared.

I slid the robe back on my shoulders and made my way into the backstage, where the next girl was already being prepped. I was in a daze, barely aware of my surroundings as I was escorted to the changing room. Before the auction began, they told us we'd be allowed an hour to prepare for our night with the highest bidder, but now, a rattled woman with a clipboard in her hands ran toward me, knitting her brows together.

"We need you in front of the building now," she barked at me.

"What? I was told I'd have an hour to get ready."

She fixed her headset and shook her head. "Mr. Kline wants you right now. There's no time for that. Tie up your robe and follow me."

With shaky hands, I redid the bow at my hip, covering up my body with the pink silk as I followed the woman outside. It was December first, and as I stepped into the chilly winter night, I trembled from the cool air and the hint of snow in the icy air.

A limousine was waiting in front of the building, and the woman wielding the clipboard ran toward it now, clicking her high heels. I followed behind, struggling in the ten-inch stilettos

I'd been told to wear for the auction. My heart was pounding as I stumbled, the woman waving me over impatiently. "Come on now, hurry! No dillydallying."

I managed to make it to the car, my heels slipping on the ice-covered road.

"Wish me luck," I muttered to the woman. In response, she merely gave me a *you-do-not-amuse-me* look, opened the door, and ushered me into the dark interior of the black limousine.

I got into the car, and the moment I sat down, the vehicle pulled away from the curb, making my heart race in expectation. The interior was all smooth, buttery black leather and tinted windows. I fumbled around for the seatbelt when the dark voice I'd remembered from the auction spoke up.

"Leave it."

I looked around, finally spotting a dark shape materializing in the seat opposite mine. We were separated by three feet of space, yet his presence still made me feel a chill right down to my bones.

"But, it's safer to... I just wanted—"

"Leave it," he repeated, firmer this time. "Quintus is a driver with decades of experience. We won't be in danger with him."

I nodded weakly before placing my hands in my lap, staring at the spot where the voice was coming from. He was still hidden in the shadows, but as we pulled out of the parking house attached to the auction building, his handsome profile came into view, rendering me speechless.

He was handsome. *Dangerously handsome.*

He didn't look at me, instead focusing his gaze on the cityscape of London as we drove away from it. I couldn't take my eyes off him, though. I was mesmerized.

"Why did you want me to come with you right away?" I demanded.

"I saw you," he answered simply. "I didn't want to wait."

"Are you…" I bit my lower lip. So many questions were on the tip of my tongue, yet I was too nervous to ask.

"Go ahead," he encouraged me with a sly smirk.

"Are you going to hurt me?" I blurted out.

He pondered my question for a moment, before nodding once, saying, "Yes. But you'll be rewarded handsomely for it."

"The payment I'm getting is meager compared to what you paid," I muttered.

"I'm not talking about that." His voice was sexy, dark and dangerous. And it was doing things to my insides I didn't want to admit.

"What then?"

"I'm talking about another offer, from me to you, Kitty."

My skin prickled when he used my nickname for *Le Cabaret*. "Do we know each other?"

"We will soon," he answered cryptically.

I reached over to the car door and opened it. He called out my nickname and lunged for me, dragging me back into the vehicle and slamming the door shut. My heart beat faster than ever as he held me in his arms.

"What the hell do you think you're doing?" I hissed.

"Saving you from your own stupidity," he scoffed, letting go of me. I retreated to my seat, my cheeks burning with embarrassment. He buckled me in himself then, careful not to touch me as he slid the seatbelt over my body.

For the next few minutes, he allowed me to stare sullenly out of the window. I had so many more questions. I needed to know what he'd meant by the offer he mentioned.

"What is your offer?" My voice was shaky as I delivered the question.

"I knew you'd ask soon enough. Well, Kitty, I'm not an evil man," Grayson told me, a wicked smirk taking over his handsome face. "I *am* a cruel one. I am offering you half of the money I paid for you today."

"Three *hundred* and seventy-five thousand?" I tried not to show my own shock as he nodded.

"That's right."

"What do I have to do for it?" Couture House was only paying me seventy-five thousand quid. It was breadcrumbs compared to the money this man was putting on the table.

"I don't want one night with you, Amicia." He reached forward, his fingers taking my chin and making me look up at him. My breath catches in my throat, waiting for his next words. "I want twenty-four of them."

"What d-do you mean?" I hadn't meant to stutter, but I was feeling weak in his presence.

"I want you to be my willing captive for twenty-four days, and twenty-four nights. You'll begin today, December first. By Christmas morning, you'll be free."

"And until then?"

"Until then..." His fingers moved down my neck, wrapping around my throat with firm pressure. "You do everything I tell you to do. You don't leave, not once, or you renounce your right to the money. You are *mine*. For twenty-four days."

I gasped as his fingers squeezed, making my mouth open and my eyes flutter as I stared up at him.

"So, what do you say, Kitty?" His voice was silky smooth and delicious like aged bourbon. "Will you be my Christmas captive?"

CHAPTER 6

Grayson

She'd said yes.

I wasn't sure whether she would. Amicia Romano was certainly different to the other girls before her. She was headstrong, with a will of her own. No one pushed my kitty around, that was for sure. I'd be the only one allowed to do that.

After she signed the papers right there in the limo, I ordered my driver to take us to the penthouse. Kai was still away running some business for me in Florida, and would only return by Christmas, so I was running short on manpower. I had a lot of work to attend to over the next week, therefore my new toy would have to learn how to be patient.

"This is where you live?" her mouth gaped open as we pulled up in front of the building. "It looks like something out of a film…" She tapped the brick wall to make sure it was real, making me chuckle.

"It's all too real, Kitty," I told her. "Now come. We have a lot of work to do before I have to return to work." I held out an arm for her, and after a moment's thought, she linked it with hers, following me into the building.

If Amicia thought the outside was impressive, the interior was sure to shock her. I was greeted by my last name by a bellboy waiting for us. He quickly gathered himself when he saw Amicia, giving her a polite nod. She stared open-mouthed as I led her to the lift. The building was decorated in art-deco style, with gorgeous glass and silver and gold accents everywhere.

The elevator took us right to the penthouse, and once the doors clicked open, I invited my new kitty inside to show her the place.

"This is the salon," I said, showing her the expansive space. "Where I greet guests. The kitchen, the dining room. This is the study. Here is the master bedroom. Down that hallway are two guest bedrooms and my home study."

"And behind here?" She knocked on a white door, making me smile. "What's behind this door?"

"That, my dear, is for me to know, and for you yet to discover." I gently took her hand in mine, leading her away from the door while she flushed. She knew what was behind that door, I knew it. But she was too shy to mention it again as I showed her to the terrace next.

I had a large wooden patio where loungers were set out when it was warm enough, overlooking the London city skyline. Now, the area was closed off, though the hot tub would still be a nice treat to enjoy on a gorgeous wintry night when the stars were out above my favorite city in the world.

By the time we returned to the salon, a group of people had gathered, and I introduced them to Amicia one by one. Sonia, the hairdresser, Neil, the makeup man, Dalia and Marigold, the seamstresses. Amicia gave me a questioning look as I ordered them all to take care of her and make her presentable.

"Am I not presentable now?" she asked, and I could hear the hint of upset in her voice. "Don't I look nice enough already?"

I approached her, my hands on her shoulders as I looked deep into her blue eyes. "You're the most beautiful woman I've ever seen. But I want you to sparkle even brighter. And I have just the thing in mind."

She gave me a doubtful look but didn't object as the team got to work. With an affectionate smile, I let them get to work while I retreated to my home office, telling Amicia I had a surprise waiting for her late at night. For the rest of the day, I busied myself with some important business, the knowledge that she was being pampered mere feet away filling me with quiet, pleasant warmth. Already, she'd managed to find her way into my heart. I was thinking about her as I worked, my thoughts spinning in circles around the gorgeous brunette that had submitted to me so freely.

I finished work hours later, hoping the team had worked their magic and that Amicia felt as pampered as she deserved to. I'd told my maid to ask her to wait in the expansive living room with a gorgeous view of the city, where I'd have a special delivery waiting for her.

As I made my way out of my office, a grin was playing on my lips—one I couldn't possibly fight off. Amicia may have been a new toy, but she'd already gotten me more excited than the last few before her. I wanted to own her. I wanted to see her submit to me, break down for me and kneel for me. I had a feeling her submission would be beautiful; something I'd treasure for the rest of my life.

She was standing with her back toward me as I made my way into the living room. Kitty was wearing a floor length, bias-cut red silk dress that wrapped around her curves in a way that made my mouth water. As she turned around, my eyes fixated on her hard nipples poking through the fabric, before going up to her perfectly made-up face.

"Kitty," I said softly. "You're a vision." I approached her, sensing her trepidation as I leaned forward to kiss her cheek. But she didn't object, not saying a word as my lips lingered against her skin. "Are you ready for your special surprise?"

"Yes." She gave me a fearful smile. The poor little thing was scared.

"Don't fear me," I said, tucking a strand of her bouncy curls behind the shell of her ear. "Don't fear me *yet*, Kitty. I'll take care of you."

She nodded; her eyes glued to mine as I clicked my fingers. The doors of the living room opened, and two men walked in carrying an enormous Christmas tree. Amicia gasped at the sight of it, then clapped her hands together in excitement, a giddy smile on her lips.

"I thought it would make it feel more like Christmas," I said with an indulgent smile. "And as a special treat, I thought we'd decorate it together."

Amicia smiled. It was an oddly intimate thing, to decorate the tree, just the two of us. But for the next hour or so, we carefully picked out the ornaments I'd ordered from an expensive boutique in town and arranged them around the tree. The smell of pine needles was thick and heady, a Christmas-scented candle burning in the background while we worked. I'd even put on some Christmas tunes, and the atmosphere was charged with tension as we worked in companionable silence.

I couldn't help but watch Kitty work her hardest to make the tree as beautiful as she possibly could. She arranged the lights and ornaments with great care, handling them with capable hands that never trembled. We were down to the star which went on top, and as she held the glittering, gilded ornament in her hands, I wrapped my arms around her waist and lifted her up so she could place it on the top of the tree.

My movement surprised her, her cheeks flushing a dark red. She didn't say anything, merely placed the star in its place to the sound of Holy Night playing on my surround-sound system, before I carefully allowed her body to slide down, pressed firmly against mine.

I could tell she was excited. Her perky nipples were straining against the silk of her dress, eager to be touched, sucked, and pinched. But I made no move to do it. I needed to earn her trust, first.

I pretended the moment hadn't happened, leaving her to her own thoughts as we finished clearing up the boxes. The tree looked magnificent in its splendor, and for the first time in years, I found myself genuinely excited about the upcoming holiday.

"I'll be doing some work in my home office now," I told Amicia, her eyes following me as I made my way across the room. *Was I imagining the longing in her gaze?* "Should you need anything, Florian is available to you."

"What about you?" Amicia asked.

"I'm not to be disturbed."

With those words, I left her alone in the expanse of the living room, smirking to myself. I knew how to play my cards right to keep her interested. Now, she'd be wondering what I was doing, eager to spend more time in my company. But I wouldn't allow her to have it, not just yet.

CHAPTER 7

Grayson

I planned for a seamstress to come to the penthouse, and my pet was fitted for a new wardrobe. Over the course of the next few days, her closet was filled with expensive designer pieces. Every day, she looked more radiant. Over the course of the first week, her transformation from a street urchin into a sophisticated woman was finalized, and even I was impressed by the results.

The first week passed peacefully, without any incidents. Initially, I'd thought Amicia would fight her captivity, resist me. But I knew what I was doing—after all, this wasn't my first time. I purposefully kept my hands off her, restraining myself even though all I'd wanted to do was to bury my cock deep with the silkiness of her pussy.

I set up a regimen for Amicia. I controlled what she ate, when she exercised. I knew of her every move in the apartment, making it my business to transform her into the perfect pet for me. Her obedience was a welcome surprise. It was as if she'd been waiting for someone to do this for her—take away any semblance of control and guide her through her life as a submissive.

I didn't touch her for a long time. I left her mostly to her own devices, not prying into what she did. She never asked to leave the penthouse. She had access to my private pool and gym in the building, and she used it with gusto, going for a swim once per day, and to work out once every other day. Florian had told me she was also using the sauna, and I'd scheduled a massage for her after her workout on the sixth day. She'd left a sweet thank you note for me through the maid, pleasing me more than she knew.

It was the seventh night of December when I decided to pay my pretty captive a visit. The guest bedroom was quiet at midnight as I stood in the doorframe, watching my Kitty sleep. Her chest was rising and falling rhythmically. She didn't suspect I was watching her, sleeping peacefully while my eyes drank in her slumbering form. She truly was breathtaking, even like this, natural and more exposed than ever. Her silk sheer nightie had ridden up, exposing inches of her tanned thighs and a sliver of the pussy I so craved to taste. But I needed to bide my time. To wait until she was ripe.

She hadn't tried to make the guest bedroom her own, but then again, she hadn't brought anything with her. The room was devoid of personal touches, but her presence in it made it beautiful.

Amicia stirred in her sleep, muttering my name which made me chuckle. At the sound of it, her eyes flew open, and she awoke with a soft sigh on her full lips. I kneeled next to her, my fingers ghosting over her cheek while she slowly came to.

"What is it?" she whispered. "Is something the matter?"

"No," I reassured her. "I thought it was about time I paid you a little visit, Kitty."

"Oh…" I witnessed goosebumps erupting over her skin, her tanned complexion flush with embarrassment. "Isn't it late?"

"Midnight," I confirmed. "I just got done with my work for the week."

"Okay," she said, sitting up straight in the bed, her eyes hungrily finding mine. "What do you want to do?"

"Well," I smirked. "I thought it was about time I tested out my new toy. Don't you think, Kitty?"

"Y-Yes," she stuttered. She painted on a confident face, but deep down, my toy was still scared of me, and I was the sick bastard who loved it.

"Good," I muttered. "We're going to test your patience tonight. I want to know you won't come without my permission."

She blanched, withdrawing her gaze as she dug her teeth into her lower lip. "Why wouldn't you let me?"

"Because I want you on edge. I want you begging for it, and I want to deny you again and again."

"Why?"

"Because," I said firmly. "It will please me. And that's the only reason you need, Kitty. You will not come until I allow it. And if you're good, there will be a special treat in it for you."

***

Amicia was proving to be a good houseguest, but there was still a lesson I had to teach her.

While she hadn't misbehaved me directly, she didn't exactly see me as an authority figure, either. And I was determined to change that. To show her that while she was staying with me for the duration of her contract, she'd obey me and do exactly as she was told. I didn't have patience for misbehaving and I had no intention of allowing her to treat me with disrespect, which made my next move necessary.

After dinner that night, I told her to wait for me in the guest bedroom. From her nervous behavior, I could tell she was afraid, and when she slipped by calling me by my first name at dinner, I realized her upcoming education was more than warranted.

I knocked on the door of her bedroom twice, and she timidly called out for me to enter.

She was sitting on the foot of the bed, fearfully raising her eyes to mine once I entered the room.

"Hello, Kitty," I spoke up. "We have an important evening ahead of us today."

"Oh?" She cocked her head to the side. "What do you mean by-"

"Lesson one," I went on, disregarding her interruption. "You don't address me as Grayson, or anything other than Sir. *Especially* when we're in the presence of others. It's a sign of respect I don't just expect from you. It's mandatory. Understood?"

Something passed over her pretty face and she set her lips into a line, finally giving me a reluctant nod.

"Good, I'm glad you understand," I smirked at her. "The second lesson. You will always treat me with respect. That does not just involve addressing me properly. I want you to be a good girl and respect me with everything you do. No talking back. No mouthing off. You treat me like your superior, because until December twenty-fifth, that's who I am."

She looked as if she was about to argue, but her lips remained pressed together. She was learning fast, which could only bode well for our future. I would make her kneel for me. I would make her beg for me. I would make her the most perfect toy for me, whatever the price.

"Tell me you'll be a good Kitty for me," I said next. "Repeat it."

"I'll be a good Kitty," she muttered, gorgeous eyes shooting daggers at me. She didn't like this. Didn't enjoy the thought of being below me. But I relished her reluctance. It would only make it that much sweeter when she finally bent the knee for me.

"Good girl. Next, for your third lesson," I went on. "You break either of those two rules, you're out of here, and I won't pay you anything."

She pursed her lips even more. Her annoyance amused me, and I fought to keep the smile off my face as she said, "I thought you wanted to get to know me better."

"Oh, darling, don't fool yourself into thinking I picked you because of your sparkling personality," I laughed, the sadist in me enjoying seeing her face fall even more. "I picked you because of your pretty face and your gorgeous body. The fact that you can dance is a nice bonus. But I don't care for your feisty streak and the way you're so damn eager to defy me. I'll get you broken in soon enough, though, but it's imperative you understand I won't accept anything but perfect obedience. Understood?"

Biting her lower lip, Amicia nodded.

"I'm going to need to hear you say it."

"Understood," she muttered.

"Understood, what?" I demanded. "What did I tell you to call me, Kitty?"

"Sir."

"So say it properly. Don't make me lose my patience."

She sighed, running her fingers through her mass of dark hair as she finally muttered, "I understand, Sir."

"Now, I'm not going to warn you again," I went on, pleased

with her level of submission already. Either she was really desperate for that money, or she was too afraid of standing up to me, knowing a punishment would be coming her way if she didn't obey. "You need to remember what I just told you for the duration of your stay. If you disappoint me, I will punish you. And my punishments aren't something you'll easily forget, so I'd suggest you stay on your best behavior."

"I understand, Sir," she repeated. I enjoyed seeing my requests hadn't made the spark in her eyes go out. I could tell she was already planning how to twirl me around her little finger, which amused me. I was in control. I wasn't going to let her spin my mind into circles as I was sure she'd done with men before. While she stayed in my home, she'd obey.

"Good girl," I said proudly. "As long as you remember your manners around me and company, we won't have a problem at all. You'll be paid as arranged."

Her eyes sparkled at the mention of money. I wondered why it was so important to her, vowing to myself to get the reason out of her sooner rather than later, if only to sate my own curiosity. I left her room then, but the fall of her shoulders didn't escape me right before I closed the door. Amicia was disappointed.

Did she want me to touch her? Was she already consumed by the desire to feel my hands on her?

I couldn't know for certain, but I did know I was already overwhelmed with the desire to make her submit.

When she would, I'd known she was mine forever. Something told me Amicia didn't kneel for just any man, which would only make the moment sweeter in my mind.

With a smirk, I closed the door of my own bedroom behind me. Soon enough, she'd join me in this room. Soon enough, she'd be more than just my Christmas captive...

CHAPTER 8

Amicia

It was late at night when the knock came. I was already in bed, tossing and turning as I wondered why Grayson hadn't come to me yet. All my senses were on high alert, and at first, I was convinced the knock was on my bedroom door.

"Yes?" I called out tentatively, pulling myself up into a sitting position. But no answer came. I shuffled my feet to the ground, bare skin touching the hardwood floors as I padded toward the door. "Who's there?"

Still, no answer. I wrapped a soft knitted cardigan around my body, teeth chattering as I made my way out of the room. The hallway was cold and quiet, but there was light at the end of it, where the front door was.

"Grayson?" I furrowed my brows and kept walking. The soft sound of voices drifted to me then, one Grayson's, the other a woman's. I felt chills go down my spine, knowing right away something was happening I wouldn't like one bit. I walked to the end of the hallway and finally saw them. Grayson, with his hand on the doorframe, preventing her from entering. She was beautiful despite her smeared makeup and the obvious fact that she'd been crying, and my stomach twisted into a thousand knots when I saw them together.

Grayson groaned, turning his head to the side. That's when he saw me, and his eyes darkened.

"What are you doing up, Amicia?" he demanded. He hadn't even used my nickname, and my shoulders fell with disappointment.

"I heard voices," I muttered, glancing between him and the beautiful woman glaring at me with pure hatred from the doorstep. "What's going on?"

"We have a little midnight visitor," Grayson explained with a tight smile. "This is Lyra. Lyra, Amicia."

She nodded at me and I repeated the motion. I didn't have it in me to give her more of a reaction, my body still twisted in knots.

"Why don't you come in, Lyra?" Grayson suggested, and I felt sick. I didn't want her here, didn't want her near the man who'd bought me. I didn't understand my own feelings but I knew they were screaming at me to get this Lyra away from Grayson. "We'll speak in my bedroom. Amicia, make us some coffee."

My lips pursed. Now he'd humiliated me to the role of a maid. I rushed toward the kitchen while Lyra gave me a self-righteous smile. My hands shook so badly I was convinced I'd break something, and in my rush to leave, I hadn't even asked them how they liked their coffee.

I prepared everything, adding sugar cubes and cream to a saucer and carrying everything over to the office. There, Grayson was sitting at his desk while Lyra sat on the armchair in front of him, wiping her eyes.

"Thank you, Kitty," Grayson spoke as I set the tray down. My heart soared when he used my nickname but I forced myself to fight the smile off my face. I was still upset. "Why don't you join us?"

"Sure," I muttered. "I'll just put some clothes on first."

"No." Grayson took me by the hand and smiled confidently. "Take the cardigan off."

"But I..." His eyes allowed no room for arguing, and I flushed lightly as I peeled off the cardigan. I shivered, not because of the cold, but because I was nervous being so exposed in front of this woman who looked very much like a booty call.

"Kneel," Grayson muttered, pointing to his feet to the side of the desk. "Next to me. Put your head in my lap."

"Please, I-"

His gaze left no chance of a reprieve, and with a sigh, I sank to my knees on the plush rug. I didn't even dare look at Lyra, instead choosing to focus on Grayson and staring up at him. I wanted him to tell her to get lost, to never come back again. I didn't want her around. I didn't want her in the space I shared with him, even if it was just for one short month. Perhaps she'd been here before—perhaps they'd dated—but I'd taken her place now, and I wasn't letting her replace me.

"Lyra," Grayson spoke up with a sigh, gently running his fingers through my hair. "Lyra, Lyra, Lyra. I told you before. I don't want you anymore. What we had is over."

So I'd been right... she'd been his lover, perhaps even his

girlfriend.

"Please." The woman leaned across his desk, pleading with him. It was excruciatingly embarrassing to watch her humiliate herself in front of him. At the same time, I was fighting the self-righteous smile off my face. "I'll do anything for you, Sir. I'll do anything you've ever wanted, give you all of me, let you have it all, Sir, please, Sir-"

"Don't call me that." Grayson's voice was devoid of emotion as he cut her off. I leaned against him, seeing the pain in Lyra's eyes as she begged for him to reconsider. But he'd already made up his mind. The only person in the room who hadn't realized it was the woman sitting in front of us. I turned my head to the side so I wouldn't have to look at her.

As Grayson told her to leave and that he didn't love her, I felt my stomach twisting. I felt sick. What did this mean for me? I was already starting to develop feelings for Grayson. But did I risk being tossed aside just like Lyra was now? Humiliated in front of his new toy while begging for a second chance?

I didn't have the answer. My lips remained tightly pressed together as Grayson said goodbye to Lyra once and for all. He closed the door firmly and told me to go back to bed. I hesitated, but his insistent gaze told me I didn't have a choice.

Burrowing back into my blankets, I chewed my bottom lip nervously as sleep evaded me for the rest of the night. I couldn't rest until I knew for certain whether he saw me as disposable. But something told me Grayson enjoyed keeping me on edge. That he'd keep me this way, enjoying my struggles. I wanted to hate him for it, but my heart betrayed me.

***

I didn't see Grayson much the next day, but he told me he'd

have a surprise for me in the evening. Some delivery men came in that afternoon, and I wasn't allowed out of the living room as they set something up.

"Are you excited for your surprise?" Grayson asked once they finally left.

"A little worried," I smiled cautiously. "Should I be afraid?"

"You should always be a little afraid around me," Grayson smirked. "Only because I love it."

The fact that he got off on my fear was thrilling, but I was too scared to bring it up. I tried to hide my flushed cheeks by allowing my hair to fall over my face. Grayson pulled his tie off the shirt he was wearing, dangling it before my eyes.

"Will you let me blindfold you?" he asked with a smile. I nodded, knowing I didn't have a choice. After all, this was what I'd signed up for. He approached me, gently wrapping the silk around my eyes. I couldn't see a thing, but he was careful as he led me down the hallway and into one of the bedrooms. He gently pulled me forward, and placed my hands on something cool. It felt like metal. With a smile, I realized what he'd done.

"If you wanted a private show, Mr. Kline," I purred. "You only needed to ask."

"I'm asking now," he muttered in my ear as he pulled off the day. The ghost of his lips sent shivers down my spine. "Will you dance for me, Kitty?"

I ran my fingers down the pole, inspecting it. It was sturdy. He'd paid money for this set up, and there was no denying my excitement. I lived to dance. To dance for Grayson would be extra special, not only because of the butterflies in my stomach. The electricity between us was sparking, and we hadn't even kissed yet.

"Let me put on some music for you, Kitty." He played with his speakers and a slow, sensual song played over the speakers.

"Now dance, pretty girl. Let me watch you twirl just for me."

I closed my eyes and allowed my mind to familiarize itself with the sound of the music. My hips started swaying. I knew he was watching me, the hot weight of his gaze following me through the room as I started twirling around the pole.

I danced for him and him alone. Finally, minutes into the dance I couldn't handle not seeing him anymore. I pulled the blindfold off but kept my eyes closed for a few precious more moments.

When I finally opened my eyes, I looked right at him. He was sitting with his legs spread, a tumbler of whiskey in one hand and a cigar in the other. I could see the outline of his erection through his slacks, and I was grateful for the sound of the music that covered up the moan that escaped my lips.

I wanted him watching me. I wanted his cock hard. I wanted him wanting me so much he'd just cut everything off and take me then and there. And if Grayson Kline wanted a personal show, I'd give him one he'd never forget.

The sound of the music reverberated through the room, through my body. I danced only for him. My dress slipped over my shoulders and I embraced it, acting coy as I slowly slipped it off. I stood before Grayson in stockings, a garter belt and a black set of lacy lingerie. I knew he was turned on. I felt the tension in the air, thick with the promise of what lay ahead. We were both prolonging this delicious moment, but I was beyond excited for the moment he finally gave me what we both wanted.

After using the pole, I crawled to him on all fours. I braced my palms on his knees, rubbing my tits over his erection and feeling him getting harder and harder.

"Don't you want to kiss me?" I whispered as I moved in closer and closer, tempting him to break the tension and just give in to the desire we both felt. "Don't you want to feel my lips on you? To make me yours?"

"You're already mine," Grayson growled, taking a long puff of the cigar and putting it out on the ashtray on the coffee table. "When I take you, you'll be begging for it. Craving it."

I didn't want to tell him I was already desperate for him. My desire for Grayson Kline grew with every second spent in his company. I found myself eager for every touch, intentional or not, and I was almost ashamed of the desire that burned within me when his fingertips so much as brushed against my skin. But he denied me on purpose. I knew it, he knew it. He wanted me to be more desperate. Usually, I'd be too embarrassed. I'd cut off contact with a man like him, a man determined to put me on my knees. Except Grayson was different. Grayson was...

He leaned forward then, and he heard my gasp as his fingers gently wrapped around my neck.

"I know you're fucking desperate for it," he muttered. "Tell me how much you want it. Tell me how badly you want me to kiss you."

"P-Please." I flushed, embarrassed by my own neediness. "Grayson, I..."

"Begging already." He smirked. "I'll only make it worse for you."

I swallowed thickly, resisting the urge to ask for more. Our lips were dangerously close together, close enough for me to smell the alcohol he'd had mixing with the mint of his toothpaste.

"Get in my bed," Grayson growled. "Right now. I want you in my arms tonight. From now on, you sleep in my bed, Kitty."

My heart swelled in my chest. Before I got the chance to pick myself up, he scooped me up in his arms and carried me to my new bedroom himself.

CHAPTER 9

Grayson

I cradled her in my arms for the rest of the night, and we woke up together in the guest bedroom. Her body was small and soft in my arms, and I cherished every breath she took as I held her. I had to resist the urge to bury my fingers in her silky depths as she slept, having to make peace with gently brushing my fingertips against her breasts instead. I wanted her. I wanted her more than I'd wanted any of the other toys. The others were merely amusement, a way to pass the time. With Kitty, it felt real.

We had breakfast together while I explained I'd taken the day off for her. She seemed excited by the idea, but there was a note of sadness in her eyes I couldn't miss, and it brought me down, too.

Finally, after we were done with breakfast, and we settled down in the living room to admire the skyline and read, I decided to address it.

"Why the sad eyes?"

She hesitated; unsure whether she should tell me the truth. Finally, her lips parted, and the words came pouring out, as if she'd waited years to answer my question. "I'm just... worried that you'll force me."

"Force you?" I repeated, raising a brow. "Force you to do what?"

"To... you know." She flushed again. "To have sex with you."

"I won't force you." My voice was gentler, kinder now. "I will make you beg for it, and I will fuck you someday, when you're ready. I'll edge you to the point you'll be begging me for more, but I'll never force you, Amicia. I told you—I'm not an evil man."

"Then why would you make me wait?" she demanded, making me smile as I touched her cheek, brushing it with my fingers.

"Because I like to watch you squirm," I muttered. "And I know you're going to be so damn beautiful when you're begging me for more."

"More what?" her words were barely above a whisper.

"More pain... more pleasure... more everything." I kissed the top of her head, finding it remarkable how attached I'd gotten to the sweet little toy after merely a week. Still, I only had two weeks left. After that, she'd be gone just like the rest of them, replaced by a new toy. *Why did the thought of it make me hurt in my chest, though?*

"You think I will enjoy it?" She sounded incredulous, making me laugh out loud.

"Oh, I know you will. Now, don't you want to know what

we'll be doing tonight if you behave yourself?"

"Yes," she nodded.

"Tell me properly, use your words." I tipped her chin back with my fingers, making her look up at me. "Make a full sentence, Kitty."

"I want to know what we'll be doing tonight if I behave myself," she muttered, blushing as she added a nearly silent "*Sir*..." at the end.

"Good girl." I felt her body tense at the two little words. They were all the same in the end. So needy, so desperate to hear their favorite praise. Kitty was just like the other girls—eager to be acknowledged, desperate to be complimented. "We're going to see the Nutcracker ballet at the London Opera House."

"W-What?" She jumped to her feet, bubbling over with excitement. "That's..."

"I'm glad you're so excited." I laughed. "The tickets are ready and there should be an outfit waiting for you. You need only behave yourself, Kitty."

"I'll behave myself," she rushed to say. "I promise... Sir."

"Good, I expect nothing less of you. Now get back to your book and I'll get back to mine. You've got something to look forward to now, don't you?"

She nodded, the faint hint of a smile not leaving her lips as she settled in the loveseat next to me. I placed a palm on her thigh, making her shiver as I grabbed her. She was my property, after all—at least for another few weeks. And I wanted to make her feel like a toy.

While we read together, I allowed my fingertips to wander all over her skin, gently smoothing down her dress. In moments, I was touching her bare skin until even I couldn't pretend I hadn't heard her whispered moans every time our skin made contact.

"You like that?" I muttered in her ear.

"Yes."

"Yes, what?"

"Yes, Sir." She blushed again.

"You want more, Kitty?"

"I do. Please. Sir."

"Remember you cannot come," I reminded her. "Not under any circumstances. Do you understand that, Kitty?"

"Yes." She nodded, her eyes gravelly burning into mine. "I won't."

"Good girl." I was going to make this hard for her, just to see how far I could push her. Once I knew how much she could take, I would erase her boundaries and set new ones in place. "Crawl between my legs."

She didn't hesitate, crawling to the spot I'd designated for her and waiting for further instructions, her hands demurely folded on her lap.

"Take my cock out," I said.

"What?" She paled at the thought. "But I… You…"

"Good toys don't argue," I reminded her. "Take it out, now."

Her shaky hands reached for me, undoing the zipper of my pants. Her fingers trembled as she touched the black silky fabric of my boxers, carefully reaching inside. Those pretty blue eyes widened when she felt how thick I was, and she pulled my cock out, a soft gasp leaving her full lips.

"Do you like it?" I muttered, and she looked up into my eyes, nodding wordlessly. "Why don't you taste it, Kitty? Maybe I'll even give you some cream to lick up."

She licked her lips and leaned forward while I put my hands behind my head, groaning as I felt her mouth wrap around my tip for the very first time.

She wasn't an experienced cock sucker—and I could tell. But I didn't mind it one bit, for what she lacked in skill, she made up for with the sheer need to please me. Her tongue twirled little circles around my tip, licking the precum out of my slit and filling her mouth with the taste of me. She moaned when my cock leaked, and I relaxed, allowing her to have full control of my hardness.

Soon, she was working me even more eagerly. Long flicks of her tongue over my length and girth made me groan impatiently. When she moved down to my balls, I buried my fingers in her long, dark mane and held on for dear life. She was getting better and better with every second that passed, so very eager to please me she would've done anything just to get her prize out of my cock.

"Amicia," I spoke up, and her eyes flitted over to mine, glazed over with wanting and need. "When I come, you won't. And you will swallow everything. I don't want you to waste a fucking drop. Is that understood?"

She nodded; her pupils dilated as she went to work my cock again. This time, I didn't hold back. I tugged on her hair hard and I held her down on me until she was sputtering and choking. With a groan, I deposited a week's worth of my cum into her throat, and pulled back, ropes of my juice dripping from her mouth onto her dress.

"Remember your promise," I told her, and she did, licking up the cum from her fingertips before scooping up more from the front of her dress. She licked up every last bit, making me grin wide. "Such a good girl you are, Amicia. You've made me very happy."

I put my cock back in my pants, my hand lingering over my pet's locks, petting her with pleasure. "We'll leave soon. You can get ready now. I want to show you off on my arm, Kitty, so make sure you look your absolute best."

She picked herself up, her skin aglow with the need to please. "You won't be disappointed, Sir."

CHAPTER 10

Amicia

If the looks I was getting at the Opera House were anything to go by, I looked better than I'd ever had.

Once I'd returned to my bedroom, I'd found a floor-length, mermaid-train red satin dress waiting for me, along with a pair of black heels with red soles. The look was completed by a black and red clutch, and jewelry that caught the light and sparkled beautifully. Grayson had attached the diamond necklace to my neck himself.

As we made our way to the Opera House, I wrapped the fur wrap I was wearing more tightly around my shoulders. I felt special when I was next to Grayson, when he looked at me as if he had a real treasure on his hands. I was a long way off from the poor orphan I used to be. In his company, I was a queen.

The thought of Margaret was heavy on my mind, reminding me with every step of the time I'd spent with the older woman.

I'd bounced from foster home to foster home when I was younger, until I finally came to stay with Margaret when I was seventeen. But if I thought the older woman would be kind and caring the way a grandmother would be, I was sorely mistaken.

From the first day I spent at Margaret's home, I was a slave. I did everything for her—I cooked and cleaned, I went grocery shopping, I massaged her feet, I ran errands. She had me quit school and take care of her full-time. And always, there'd be the promise on her thin lips—I'd inherit the apartment when she died. A worthy payment for all the years I'd spent waiting for her hand and foot.

Margaret was sick, she had been since I'd first met her. I prepared cocktails of drugs for her every night, and she never got better, but she never got much worse, either. And before I knew it, I'd turned eighteen, and she'd emotionally blackmailed me into staying longer. What else was I supposed to do? I had no money, no education, and no future. Taking care of Margaret was my only option. And every time she hit me for not being fast enough with her requests, I told myself it would all be worth it in the end, when she'd be—as she used to say—relieved from the constant pain. Then, I would inherit the apartment, and I could finally start taking dance lessons Margaret had always refused to pay for.

Except as it turned out, Margaret had lied to me from the start.

She passed away six months before I started dancing at *Le Cabaret*, and the apartment she'd promised me turned out to be a rented property, not her own. Not only was I thrown out of it within days of Margaret's passing, but I also found out the only thing I'd inherited was a debt of ten thousand pounds.

I'd spent four years convincing myself she loved me, but in the end, she delivered the worst blow of all. And to top it all off, I knew her dying was my fault and nobody else's. A fact I'd have to live with for the rest of my life.

I'd had no choice but to start dancing at *Le Cabaret.* I spent painstaking hours on stage to repay the woman's debt, living with the guilt of her death hanging above me. Some days, I wished I'd died instead of her. It was certainly what I deserved.

My thoughts were swimming with Margaret and her demise as Grayson and I made our way to the Opera House. He could tell I was distracted, but didn't bother me, allowing me to be alone with my thoughts.

But as soon as the performance started, I was hooked, forgetting about my problems if only for an hour or two.

The performance of the Nutcracker had me mesmerized. Grayson had given me a pair of opera glasses, and I watched the production in detail from our balcony seats. We had a private area reserved solely for us, and we had a wonderful view of both dancers and the audience.

I was grateful that Grayson allowed me to watch the ballet without interruption. Sometime in the middle of the ballet, his hand snuck to my knee, gently parting the satin of my dress, and holding onto my leg with firm fingers. His touch sent shivers down my spine, making me even more excited for what was to come. I wanted him to touch me more. I was eager to keep playing with him, but Grayson didn't make a move to continue our game from earlier. I kept my eyes focused on the stage, watching the ballerinas twirl.

Once it was time for the intermission, Grayson gave me a curious look, asking, "You love the ballet, don't you?"

"I do," I admitted, glancing at him with a small smile playing on my lips. "I've always wanted to be a dancer."

"A ballerina."

"Yes."

"So why not do it?"

I laughed bitterly. It was all so easy for him. If he wanted something, all he had to do was pay for it. "I never had the money. I learned by myself and went to many, many auditions. But they never gave me a role."

His brows furrowed as he stared at me. "I want you to dance for me tonight."

"The way I did at *Le Cabaret*?" I muttered.

"No," he shook his head firmly. "The way you *want* to dance. The way you *love* to dance."

My eyes lit up as I looked up at him. He'd just made me happier than he could possibly know. "Thank you, Sir."

"That's quite alright, Kitty. It will be enjoyable for me. Now, would you like a drink or a snack?"

I nodded, and he led me out of our private seating area and ordered a bottle of champagne for us. My eyes glittered as he presented me with a flute of bubbly, and I filled my belly with the sparkling drink. Grayson had some too, also getting me a heart-shaped box of chocolate pralines before we returned to our seats.

"This isn't part of my diet," I teased him as he presented me with the box.

"I like spoiling you," he shrugged with a mischievous look. "It won't hurt. And you'll dance for me when we get home, so I'm sure you'll work it off."

While we'd been in the main area of the Opera, I'd noticed people staring at us. There were some eyes on me, but mostly, it was Grayson who held everyone's attention. I was quickly coming to realize just how important and influential he was. These people respected him, and what was more, it seemed every person in the building knew his name. I was impressed.

For the rest of the ballet, Grayson's hand snuck back up my knee, this time inching closer and closer to the spot between my legs that was so very eager for his touch. But he never touched it, not even brushing his fingers against it once.

Finally, when the performance was over, I clapped louder than anyone else in that room. I stood up with a bright smile, impressed by the wonderful performance. I was deeply grateful to Grayson for bringing me there, and once we left the room in the company of an employee, my hand snuck into his, and I intertwined my fingers with his, squeezing his palm gently. Our eyes met. I didn't have to say a word—he knew I was grateful, and his smile told me he was proud of me.

In the lobby of the opera, people milled in small groups. Grayson held everyone's attention. I noticed men and women alike watching us closely, and it filled me with a strange sense of pride.

I thought I saw a familiar face in the crowd, and I had to do a double take to make sure. But there was no doubt about it. Capri, the *Le Cabaret* dancer who'd told me about Couture House was there, in the presence of a familiar-looking man in his fifties with a shock of dark grey hair.

She spotted me too, and her worried expression stretched into a smile. But her face fell the next moment as the man seemed to notice her attention had shifted. He reprimanded her, grabbing her by the arm and making me wonder how hard his grip was when Capri winced.

"Seen someone you know?" Grayson muttered in my ear, and I nodded, turning to face him.

"My friend, Capri," I said. "She's the one you should thank for making me go to Couture House in the first place."

"Well then," he smiled broadly. "We might as well head over

there and thank her now. I trust you recognize the man with her, too?”

“I don’t,” I muttered, feeling ashamed. Was I supposed to recognize him? “Who is he?”

Grayson smiled widely at me. “He’s the other man who almost outbid me at your auction. Come, let’s say hello.”

My smile faded. I remembered the gray-haired man then, sitting in the audience as I stood up on the stage in the auction house in Notting Hill. I wasn’t exactly thrilled about saying hello to him, but Grayson’s lecture on obedience was still too fresh on my mind for me to disagree.

I meekly followed him to the other end of the room where Capri’s smile grew once she saw us nearing her.

“Capri!” I exclaimed, hugging her close. Her body was stiff under my embrace, as if she were nervous to display any kind of affection toward me. But her eyes spoke volumes, and I was worried to see signs of pain in her once innocent gaze.

“It’s so good to see you,” she whispered in my ear when I pulled back from the hug. “So good.”

“Kline,” the man with her spoke coolly, but his interest shifted to me after the greeting. “Is this the little toy you picked up for yourself the other day? No, it can’t be.”

“Indeed it is,” Grayson replied with a smooth smile, proprietorially wrapping an arm around my waist. I felt shivers go down my spine when he touched my exposed back. “Finding it hard to believe?”

“Well, she looks much better,” the older man chuckled. “She was nothing more than a street urchin at the auction.”

My smile fell. The man was rude, and I didn’t enjoy his leering gaze as he devoured my body with his eyes. I didn’t like what he’d said about me. As if I was worth nothing before Grayson got his hands on me.

"From what I remember," I spoke up. "You were more than eager to get your hands on me even when I was *just* a street urchin."

"Doesn't she have a mouth on her," the older man smirked, ignoring me as if I were just a useless toy. "You'll have to clip that tongue, Kline. Or maybe I could discipline her myself."

"No," Capri cut in. "Please don't."

"Did I ask you a question?" the man hissed.

"No, Sir, I'm sorry, but-"

"Then shut up." His tone left no room for arguing and I paled at the way he treated her. I was grateful when Grayson's arm pulled me in closer.

"We'll be leaving now," he said, nodding at the older man. "Until next time."

"Goodbye," I whispered at Capri, knowing her tortured gaze would follow me into my dreams. "I hope I'll see you again soon."

She merely nodded as Grayson led me away. I was too scared to bring up the man or Capri again, but I could tell by his troubled expression, the older man's mistreatment of my friend hadn't escaped Grayson, either.

The ride back home in Grayson's limousine was quiet and charged with electricity. He didn't take his eyes off me once, staring intently as we drove back to the penthouse. I knew whatever was coming when we returned would include him stripping my clothes off and edging me until I begged for release. There were still a few hours to go, hours where I wouldn't be allowed to come, and I had a feeling Grayson would take the time to torture me so beautifully I'd be desperate for more.

I wasn't wrong. The moment we arrived back in the penthouse, he undid his bowtie, his eyes devouring me as he said, "Finally alone, Kitty. Join me in front of the locked door in the hallway in ten minutes. Keep on your lingerie, the jewels, and the shoes. Your hair and makeup exactly the way it is now."

I nodded, feeling goosebumps erupt all over my skin as I closed the door to my bedroom, leaning against it with my back. Carefully, I peeled the red satin dress off me, taking a long, critical look at my body in the floor-length mirror in my room. I looked good—possibly better than I'd ever looked.

Minutes later, I waited for Grayson in front of the door I'd questioned him about the first time I came to his home. My nerves were getting the better of me, and I was trembling in anticipation when he arrived, his eyes filled with dark intent.

"Hello, Kitty," he said in his gravelly, sexy voice. "Are you ready to play?"

"Yes, Sir," I quipped.

He took an old-fashioned gold key from his pocket and unlocked the door. Curiously, I peeked inside the room, but it was dark. Grayson turned on the dimmed lights a moment later, and my eyes widened in surprise.

It was a playroom, but it certainly wasn't meant for children. The room had an enormous black and red round bed with a fur throw on it, and several pieces of equipment my imagination quickly worked out to be meant for sex. I felt myself blushing deeply, but I didn't have a moment to consider what was happening, as Grayson's fingers wrapped around mine and he invited me deeper into the dark room.

"Welcome," he muttered. "I've been waiting to bring you here, Kitty. I think you're going to love it."

"Yes, S-Sir." I couldn't help stuttering, my nerves getting the best of me yet again. "What do you want me to do?"

"Everything," came his reply, accompanied by a devilish grin. "Except come, of course."

Moments later, he'd explained most of the furniture in the room, sending shivers of embarrassment and excitement all over my body. My blood was pumping with adrenaline. I wanted him to do things to me. To hurt me, to pleasure me, to bring me so close to the brink I'd be begging for more. Grayson seemed to sense my feelings, and he gently guided me to the bed, ordering me to lie on my back.

"Worry not, my Kitty," he spoke up in a low growl. "I won't use any of those on you tonight. It's too soon. This night is all about you."

I was relieved and disappointed at the same time, but I trusted his judgement. Grayson's fingers slid over my body with appreciation, and I trembled beneath his touch. He slid my thong down my hips, exposing my needy pussy which had been waxed nearly bare, according to his instructions.

"I'm so fucking tempted to taste you," he muttered. "But first, you have to dance for me."

"There's no music," I managed weakly, but he merely smiled and clicked his fingers. The sound of the piano filled the room as if by magic. "Well, that will do..."

"Do you need anything else? Shoes?"

"No," I shook my head. "This is enough."

"Then by all means, Kitty," he smirked. "The floor is yours."

I stood up, taking a deep breath as I waited for the music to wash over me. I remembered the dance I'd performed at my last audition, allowing the memory of it to put me back on the stage where I'd never danced before. I made the music my own and began to dance. Classical ballet moves mixed with my own creations to form a dance designed to seduce Grayson Kline into giving me everything I'd ever wanted.

While I danced, I felt his gaze on me, eyes following me as I moved through the room, thirstily drinking me in as I twisted my body this way and that. The music carried into another concerto, faster, with a quicker pace. My steps picked up too, and I was twirling on the floor until I came crashing to my knees in front of Grayson at the very end of the song.

"That was beautiful," he told me with a hoarse voice. "You're a very good dancer, Kitty. Classically trained?"

"Not yet," I shook my head.

"I could tell."

"Oh?" My face fell instantly.

"Your dance may lack the educated moves, but you make up for it with passion." He smiled at me with affection. "How come you never trained as a dancer?"

"I could never afford it."

His face softened at the sound of my words. "I'm sure that will change after your pay day."

"I hope so." I allowed myself to smile. "Now I just have one request, Sir."

He sat back in his armchair while I picked myself up. "What's your request, Kitty?"

I smiled, saying, "I want you to dance with me, Sir."

"Oh..." He hesitated, pondering my words. But I saw something inside him shift, and he seemed to change his mind. "Okay then. Let's do it."

"Do you know the steps to the waltz?"

"Yes."

"Then what are you waiting for? Let's dance," I smiled wide.

I hadn't danced with many men, but from the way Grayson held my body, I knew he was confident in his movements, confident enough to spin me on the hardwood without slipping up once.

I looked up at him with admiration. "You're not half bad. Where did you learn?"

"I had to learn," he smiled as he held me close. "Part of being a gentleman."

He was confident and suave, and his grip on me was just firm enough to assert his dominance over me. I leaned into him and he took note, smiling with growing warmth in his eyes. When his lips turned up, I found myself staring at his mouth, wondering when he would finally break this tension and kiss me.

I was eager to ask, eager to know. But I forced myself to stop before the question could float from my lips. Still, from the amused look on Grayson's face, I knew he'd guessed what I was wondering about.

As the music reached its crescendo, he leaned in closer. Now his mouth was an inch away from mine. I could feel his minty, cool breath on my lips, and my tongue darted out, licking at the remains of his exhale.

"You're so desperate, aren't you, Kitty?" he asked, his voice hoarse. "Wondering when I'm going to kiss those pretty, full lips..."

"I wasn't," I defended myself weakly, and he just chuckled, knowing as well as I did that I was lying through gritted teeth. "I was just-"

"Maybe I should," he went on. "I want to know if you taste as good as you smell..."

His lips brushed mine then and I froze mid-song, shivering in his arms. "What are you doing?"

"Savoring you," he muttered before touching his lips to mine again. "And goddamn, you taste incredible, Kitty..."

I couldn't take it anymore. Wrapping my arms around his neck, I pulled him in against mine, deepening our kiss. I could feel the ghost of his smile against my mouth as he responded, his cock jumping between us as I pushed my tongue into his mouth.

He tasted like every dream I'd ever had coming true. I couldn't get enough. My body melted into his embrace and I allowed his hands to explore my body while we kissed. He grabbed my ass, making me shriek as he carried me over to the bed in the room.

"I'm not just going to taste your lips tonight," he muttered against my lips.

I was too far gone to speak. Not trusting my voice, I blushed as a moan tore itself from my lips and Grayson explored my body with his tongue, fingers and eyes. I writhed beneath his watchful gaze and he caged my body, climbing on top of me on the bed.

"Perfect," he muttered as he watched me squirm beneath him. "So breathtakingly perfect."

I blushed as he leaned over me, his mouth kissing a line from my lips down my chin, neck, to my chest and then ever lower. I was eager, desperate for his touch, raising my hips to meet his lustful lips and making him chuckle. I wanted so much more.

Finally, Grayson's lips touched my pussy and I mewled in surprise. I hadn't done anything like that before. Hadn't ever had a man lick me, kiss me... *there*. It felt incredible, and Grayson's touch was that of an expert, bringing me closer and closer to pleasure as I quivered beneath him.

"Remember your promise, Kitty," he reminded me. "No coming."

I whimpered. It was harder than he thought—or perhaps this was the goal of his cruel little game, to push my every boundary until I was begging him for the sweet release of an orgasm. But he'd treated me so well that day, given me everything I'd ever dreamed of, and I wanted to give him back the pleasure he'd offered me. I restrained myself, reduced to a mess of moans as he continued his gentle assault on my body.

His lips were everywhere, his tongue parting my folds and kissing every hidden part of me. My eyelids fluttered open and closed in an effort not to come on his tongue. It was impossibly hard to hold it, but every time Grayson felt me getting close, he pulled back with a devilish grin on his lips. He loved torturing me, and I loved his cruel touch against my skin.

His touch was something between a punishment and a reward. The way he licked me spoke of years of experience, and a sudden bout of jealousy had me clenching my fingers in his salt-and-pepper hair. I wanted him. I wanted to sleep with him. I wanted to come for him. But I kept my promise, like I'd told him I would, allowing Grayson to torture my body with pleasure.

I was a shaky mess by the time he was done, his erection pressing painfully against my stomach as he looked up to look at me.

"Your time is almost up, Kitty," he told me. "Twenty minutes and you get to come. Can you abstain a little while longer?"

I nodded, gritting my teeth, and he went back between my legs, this time adding a finger to the torture, sliding in and out of my wetness. I'd never been more desperate for anything. I counted down the minutes, and when Grayson caught me doing it, he made me count down out loud.

"Ten," I whispered, my body so close to the edge a lick of his tongue would send me overboard. "Nine. Eight. Oh God, Sir…"

"Keep counting," he grunted, licking my clit until I clasped my legs around his neck, holding him in place.

"Seven. Six. Five. Four."

My eyes were rolling back, my body ready for the release I was craving so very desperately. Grayson didn't ease up, making every second of the time I had left unbearable.

"Three…"

He bit the inside of my thigh, making me cry out with pain and barely held back pleasure.

"Two. Please, Sir!"

He sucked my pussy into orgasm the moment that last number left my lips.

"One…"

I came apart beneath him, my body arching with desperation as he licked my cream. I came while crying his name, my fingers tangled in his hair and my eyes locked with his dark gaze.

I should have known then and there that I already belonged to Grayson Kline.

CHAPTER 11

Grayson

"**W**e're going to have company tonight," I told Amicia as we sat down to dinner.

"Oh?" She raised her brows, but didn't ask further questions before dabbing daintily at her lips and setting her napkin down. "Will you need me with you, Sir?"

"No," I shook my head. "It's a business partner that's coming over, we have an important matter to discuss. Actually, you might remember him."

"Who is it?" Her eyes sparkled with interest. She hadn't seen many of my partners apart from Florian who was a regular around the apartment. With Kai still being away, she hadn't even met him yet.

"We met him at the opera, remember?" I set my napkin down too. "The man who was with your friend."

"Oh, him." Her expression fell in an instant, making me chuckle.

"I take it you didn't take much of a liking to him."

"No, Sir." She shook her head vehemently. "He seemed very full of himself. And I didn't like the way he was treating my friend."

I hadn't cared for how rough he'd been with his plaything either, but I didn't mention that to Amicia. It would only make her more nervous about him being in the same apartment.

"Is she coming with him?" She asked next, a hopeful look on her face.

"No, this is a business meeting."

"What about, Sir?"

I gave her a curious look. Amicia never asked much about my business, though I could sense she was interested. She was probably worried about probing me too much and asking questions I didn't want to give her the answers to. But in the moment, I found myself strangely eager to divulge more information.

"We are entering a new business venture together," I explained. "He's coming over so we can drill down the details. I asked him to come here because I didn't want to leave you alone."

"Thank you, Sir." Kitty's eyes sparkled and I smiled as she asked to be excused from the table.

"You may go. Actually..." I tapped a finger against my chin. "I may want you to be present at the meeting after all."

"Isn't it a business meeting?" she asked, cocking her head to the side. "I don't think I'd be much help, Sir..."

She was obviously trying to get out of it, which amused me

at the same time as it played to the sadist in me. A part of me wanted to see her squirming in front of my business associate, Ilan Gibbons. His name carried a certain weight in the city, but while he looked clean on the outside, he got his hands dirtier than I ever had.

"I'd like you to keep me company," I told her with a wicked grin. "I might get bored. So you'll be kneeling at my feet while he pays us a visit. I'll surely enjoy his jealousy when he sees you again, too."

"But, Sir-"

"Yes?" I cut her off sharply, my eyes daring her to go on. Amicia swallowed, shaking her head without another complaint. She was getting better at obeying me, which pleased me. I dismissed her, telling her to be in my office ten minutes before Gibbons was set to arrive, and to wear something that would please me.

I had an after dinner whiskey while my toy got ready, and didn't get the chance to check whether she was waiting, because the bell rang a couple moments early. I let the doorman handle Gibbons, my mouth forming a thin line as I waited for the lift. The man was already trying to intimidate me with his early appearance, but I'd be damned if I let him.

The elevator doors opened and Ilan Gibbons sauntered out with a wide grin. He looked good, always had, but I knew there was pure evil lurking underneath his exterior.

"Good to see you, Gibbons," I muttered. "Care for a drink?"

"Have your maid make me an Old Fashioned," he nodded. "Where's your office? And more importantly, where's that pretty little captive of yours?"

Ignoring his words, I guided him to the office. Amicia was nowhere to be seen and my mind raged at her disobedience. I mixed Gibbons a drink at the bar myself, ignoring his quips about how short-staffed I was. It wasn't like I couldn't afford a maid, I just valued my privacy. The less people around, the fucking better, as far as I was concerned.

Moments after I joined Gibbons at my desk, there was a timid knock at the door which could only mean one thing. I called for Amicia to enter. The door opened, and she stood on the doorstep in a red leather corset with white fur lining, and matching red velvet gloves. Around her neck was a velvet ribbon with a bell. I smiled at the sight of her.

"A little late, aren't we?" I asked her, bemused.

"I'm sorry, Sir. Let me make it up to you." Amicia smiled wide, dropping to her knees and seductively crawling closer to me until she settled on a plush white pillow by my feet. I'd almost managed to forget about Gibbons until the pervert spoke again.

"Doesn't seem like your toy is very well trained," he grumbled. "Disobeying you already, is she? If you'd like to teach the girl a lesson, I'd be more than happy to help. I know you young men are stingy with the pain you dole out, but I'm certainly not afraid to slap a bitch."

Amicia crawled closer to me, glaring at my business associate.

"I assure you, I'm perfectly capable of disciplining Kitty myself," I told him with a firm smile. Absent-mindedly, I ran my fingers through Amicia's hair. I could tell I was making old Gibbons jealous, and it fucking pleased me. I wanted him squirming in his seat, realizing what he'd missed out on.

"Shall we get straight to business?" I suggested. "As far as the SoHo area goes, I've debated-"

"There's something I should say before," Gibbons interrupted, holding his hand up. I gritted my teeth. I didn't take well to being interrupted, especially by sleazy men like him who thought they had the world by the balls. "I'm backing out of the deal."

My mouth thinned and Amicia slid even further behind my

chair, sensing the shift of mood. "You can't back out, Gibbons. The papers have already been signed."

"I'll make it work," he waved his hand dismissively before a wicked smile overtook his face. "Unless of course, you're willing to renegotiate."

"We've already discussed and signed off on the details," I hissed.

"Well, unfortunately for you, I changed my mind," Gibbons smirked, setting his eyes on Amicia. "You have something I want and I am unwilling to work with you until you... *share it*, at the very least."

"What are you talking about?"

"Your little captive, of course." He leaned forward. I prayed he wouldn't attempt to touch my Kitty, because if he tried, it would not end well for him. "I should've bid higher. I realize that now. But I'm giving you an option—sell her to me before the end of your contract. I'll pay good money."

Amicia's fingers dug into my leg as I shook my head. "She's not for sale."

"Everyone has a price," Gibbons drawled. "I'm sure your *Kitty* does too." He grinned when he saw the worry etched on my face. "Oh yes, I've done my research. Amicia Romano is her real name. A wannabe dancer."

"You had no right-" Amicia spoke up, but I gently took her shaky hand in mine and pulled her back.

"I'll handle this," I told her calmly before turning my attention back to Gibbons. "While I appreciate your sudden interest in my toy, it is neither welcome nor warranted, as she will never belong to you."

"That's up to her." Gibbons leaned back in his chair without a care in the world. "I think she should be the one to decide, don't you?"

"I don't want anything to do with you," Amicia barked from her half-hidden position.

"Oh but darling, think of the money." Gibbons' eyes sparkled as he leaned forward. "I could make you rich."

"I don't want your money," Amicia muttered.

"That settles it as far as I'm concerned," I added pointedly. "She's not fucking interested. If you strike a deal with the girl after December twenty-fifth, that's up to her. But while she's mine, you will not touch her."

"Then you can kiss your deal goodbye," Gibbons delivered the punchline we'd all been waiting for. "The copy with my signature has... ah, mysteriously disappeared." He smirked. "How convenient for me."

"If you want to play dirty, that's fine with me, Ilan," I told him. "Just know you're playing by my rules now."

I stood up, buttoning my blazer, and he followed suit, eyes flashing with anger. He was seemingly so convinced I'd accept his offer, he seemed shocked I was already done with the conversation.

"Need I remind you our lack of collaboration will cost you?" he spoke up viciously. "Are you really trying to complicate your own life even further, Kline?"

"No," I smiled broadly. "I'm just trying to put the trash where it belongs."

He gasped, the color draining from his face while Amicia giggled behind us. "I will not be spoken to like that."

"And what are you going to do about it?" I smirked. "You may run the legalities around here, but I can have you dead within the night."

"Are you threatening me?"

"Yes," I grinned. "What are you going to do about it?"

After a moment of silence, he hammered the desk with his fist. "You haven't heard the end of this, Kline. And you'll wish you'd agreed to my terms the next time I come here."

"I don't have regrets," I told him. "And I'm not about to start because of you. Now, if you'd be so kind and get the fuck out."

The man stormed out of his office, and I watched him smash the elevator button with his finger. He gave me one last pissed-off look before the doors closed and the lift began its descent.

My argument with Gibbons would cost me months of work. But there was nothing to be done. He'd offended my Kitty, and threatened me. He was lucky he'd gotten out alive. Most men of his stature and age were wise enough not to try and provoke me. Gibbons would just have to find out the hard way why that was.

"Are you okay?" I helped Amicia to her feet. "You're shivering. Are you cold?"

"No, that guy just gives me the creeps," she muttered. "Is he gone?"

"Yes, and he isn't coming back." I ran my hands down her ice-cold forearms. "You're freezing. It's too cold in here for this adorable Miss Sexy Santa outfit."

She grinned despite herself, doing a little twirl for me. "You like it?"

"You look perfect, Kitty," I assured her. "How about you give me a little private show in the playroom?"

Her eyes sparkled with delight. "I would love that, Sir."

"Perfect," I smirked. "Then what are you waiting for? Get that little ass in the room so I can put some marks on it..."

She seemed scared by the thought and yet she smiled, heading straight for the playroom. My mind unfolded with dark possibilities of what I could and would do to her in the room. One thing was certain. Everything Gibbons wished he could do to Amicia, I would end up doing to spite him tonight.

CHAPTER 12

Grayson

week had passed since I'd taken my newest playthings to the Opera. With Kai being gone, I'd been consumed by the tasks I needed to complete to keep my business in check. I didn't have much time to spend with Amicia, and she seemed to understand that I was a busy man. Still, the sad look in her eyes didn't escape me. Those days, the only time I got to spend with her was sitting down to dinner together. It was my favorite part of the day, marred only by the sadness in her eyes.

I made sure she had enough to do. She still exercised daily in my private gym and went for regular swims and sauna visits.

I'd gotten a dance instructor for her at the gym, which she'd been delighted by. I also scheduled massages for her twice weekly, along with beauty treatments and salon visits. She always looked perfect, like a refined version of the girl I'd first seen in *Le Cabaret*.

That night, it was a week since I'd made her come with my mouth on her sweet little cunt, and I was eager to have more of her. We were sitting down to dinner again, and my toy was unusually quiet, unwilling to meet my eyes. I asked her question after question, but only received one-word answers in response. I understood she was lonely, but this was no way for a kept pet to act, and I was going to tell her as much.

Her knife made scratching noises against the china as she ate, the only sound in the quiet room.

"Are we going to spend some time together tomorrow?" she asked, making me look up at her.

"Aren't you forgetting something?"

Her eyes narrowed. "Are we going to spend some time together tomorrow, *Sir*?" she asked, the hint of snarkiness obvious in her voice.

"If I can find the time," I replied, returning to my food.

I could feel her staring at me, but I refused to acknowledge it. She was being a very bad toy, and I couldn't tolerate her misbehaving.

"You're neglecting me." Her voice was defiant, tinted with sadness.

"How so?"

"I've been alone this whole time." She put down her fork and crossed her arms, glaring at me. "You don't even pay attention to me anymore. What's the point of paying all this money to keep me if you aren't even doing anything with me?"

"That's not a question you should ask," I told her plainly. "I don't appreciate you meddling in my affairs, Amicia."

"I'm not meddling," she hissed. "I'm just wondering what I've done to upset you this much."

"Upset me? You haven't upset me."

"But you don't even look at me anymore!" she cried out, sweeping her arm over the table, and knocking over her own plate. We both watched as the porcelain crashed to the ground, breaking into pieces and slivers of white, shiny material. Amicia's lower lip trembled. "I'm sorry, I didn't mean to..."

I didn't respond, just rubbed my temples. "That wasn't a wise thing to do, Amicia."

"It doesn't matter. Nothing does."

"Nothing?" I'd had enough. She'd pushed my limits long enough. "Apologize."

"Apologize, to you?" she laughed bitterly. "No, I don't think I will."

"Apologize," I demanded again, glaring at her. "Now."

She seemed to understand I was serious, and she got the word out through gritted teeth. "Sorry."

"Apologize properly."

"I'm sorry, Sir." She was angry now, and I knew it would soon be time for me to discipline her. "It's just a plate. And it seems like the damn thing matters more to you than I do."

I gritted my teeth together as I stared her down. "It's not just a plate. It was part of my mother's dowry. It's been in our family for generations. As for your second accusation, Kitty, I'm sure you know just as well as I do, you're wrong. You're my property, just like the plate. And you sure aren't acting like it, which I don't like."

My words shut her up, and her lips formed a line as she stood up, getting on her knees, and scooping up the pieces of the broken plate.

"Leave it," I demanded, but she paid me no mind, still

sweeping up the broken porcelain. The inevitable happened moments later and she hissed, a long slit opening on her left ring finger, blood dripping all over the hardwood floor.

I kneeled next to her, and she sheepishly allowed me to wrap a silk handkerchief embroidered with my initials around her hand. I stopped the bleeding and guided her back to her chair.

"Does it hurt?" I asked, and she shook her head, refusing to meet my gaze.

"Not anymore."

"It's not too deep, so it shouldn't need stitches," I muttered, and Kitty nodded. "Amicia."

Finally, she looked up at me. From my tone, she seemed to realize I was angry, and she shrank back in fear, as if she were afraid I was going to slap her.

"You disobeyed me," I reminded her. "You broke a prized possession and hurt yourself in the process. You *do* understand you need to be punished, don't you, Kitty?"

She nodded; her eyes boring into mine. The fear was there, making her terrified, and making me wonder how she'd been punished before she'd met me.

"I'm not going to hurt you permanently," I promised her. "You have my word. But I cannot allow you to act this way, as if my orders mean nothing at all. Do you understand, Kitty?"

"Yes, Sir," she managed to get out.

"Now," I went on. "Will you tell me why you've been so upset over the past few days?"

"I..." She swallowed. I knew she didn't want to admit she was starting to feel things for me, and I also knew I shouldn't have been pushing her, because I had nothing to offer her in return for her feelings. Yet I couldn't help myself. I was the sadistic prick who wanted everything from her, giving nothing back. "I've been feeling lonely. You've been very busy."

"I have a business to run, Amicia," I reminded her.

"I know. But... I wish you had more time to spend with me. I thought... I thought we'd spent every minute of the twenty-four days together."

So had I. Before Kai had to leave. "I'm sorry, Kitty."

She nodded, looking away again and filling me with worry I wasn't used to. "It's okay."

"It's not," I spoke up again. "I will make it up to you. We'll go out tonight. I'm taking you to dinner. And afterward, I'll punish you for tonight."

Her eyes, which had momentarily lit up with pleasure, were wary again. "Punish me?"

"Of course," I went on smoothly, motioning toward the broken plate. "You've disappointed me, Kitty. I'm ready to make up for my own mistakes, but you must pay for yours too. Worry not. It will be a fun evening. Wait for me in front of the lift at seven p.m."

"Yes, Sir." She smiled tentatively and I kissed her forehead.

"Good girl."

***

She wore a silver glittering gown made of sequins that evening, and a pair of barely there, sky-high heels. I'd made her take lessons with the designer who made them, who taught her how to walk in the shoes.

Amicia looked like a vision that night—her hair sleek in a tall ponytail, her face made-up and her body glittering from the shimmering, scented powder I'd asked the makeup artist to apply. We were going out for a night on the town, at one of my favorite restaurants in Notting Hill called Carpe Diem.

I wrapped a sheer shawl around her shoulders, but I hadn't

complimented my toy. Her transgression was still on my mind, and she hadn't done anything to make up for it yet.

I guided her down the lift to the limousine, and then from the car to the restaurant. I felt several pairs of eyes on us as we made our way to our table. She looked breathtaking, and I was certain many men in that room were jealous of my prized possession.

We were just sitting down when I heard a delighted shriek, someone saying my name. I turned around to see Dylan Benson squealing in delight.

"Dylan!" I said with pleasure. "What a wonderful surprise. What are you doing here?"

The gorgeous redhead pecked both of my cheeks, admiring me with her green eyes while Amicia stared her down with a venomous glare. "I'm here with my fiancé, Winston Clare. Winston, come meet Grayson!"

A man about my age, handsome and charming, approached us, grinning when he saw me. "Ah, you must be Grayson Kline. The man I have to thank for my wife-to-be."

"None other," I said with a wide grin, shaking the man's hand. "And this is Amicia, my date."

"What a beauty," the man muttered, shaking Kitty's hand. Dylan kissed her cheek, making Amicia blush.

"She really is," Dylan gushed. "So wonderful to see you here, Grayson. Would you like to join us for dinner?"

I could feel the disappointment oozing from Amicia as I smiled politely at Dylan. "I would love to—but I promised my wonderful date to spend the night making her feel special. Raincheck?"

Dylan's eyes flashed with jealousy, then sparkled even brighter as she leaned in to tell Amicia, "You really are lucky, my friend. Grayson never puts his playthings first—I should know! You must be very special, very special indeed."

We said our goodbyes, and the couple left us to sit down at our table. I busied myself by unfolding my napkin, feeling Amicia's eyes on me.

"Who was she?" she asked, unable to stop herself. "The woman... Dylan. Who was she, Sir?"

"A former plaything of mine," I replied, my eyes boring into my date's. "I kept her for a few weeks last year."

"Oh," Amicia muttered. "And she's now engaged to someone else?"

"Of course," I went on. "I'm glad she's happy."

"Aren't you..." She bit her lower lip as the maître'd placed the menus on the table in front of us. "Jealous?"

"Of that Clare man?" I chuckled. "Of course not, Kitty. I let go of Dylan for a reason. This way is better for her, and for me. Otherwise I wouldn't be sitting here with you."

This seemed to appease her, and she smiled brightly as I ordered for both of us.

We were halfway through our dinner when she asked about Dylan again. "Did you love her?"

I didn't need to ask who she meant. I pondered her question, though there was really only one answer I could give her. "No, I did not."

"Why not?"

I gave her a curious look. She was a curious little pet, which amused me. Still, she was prying about things she had no business asking about. "Aren't you asking a lot of questions tonight, Kitty. I didn't love her because I've never loved anyone."

"Never?" she wondered.

"No. Have you been in love before, Amicia?"

She gave a noncommittal shrug. "There was a boy... when I was still living with the woman who was my foster parent..."

"You loved him?"

"Maybe," she muttered. "I'm not sure."

"You know what they say," I went on. "If you aren't sure, you haven't been in love."

"Oh, I have," she went on in a soft whisper.

"Oh?" I repeated before my eyes flashed with understanding. "Oh, I see."

She didn't respond save for the flush of her cheeks as she continued with her dinner.

We didn't speak up again until we were done with our meal. Then, I escorted Amicia from her seat and told her we'd take a quick walk around town to see some Christmas decorations before returning home.

She delighted in seeing the lit-up trees all over Notting Hill, and we were having a wonderful time, our squabble from lunch forgotten, though her punishment was still on my mind. We were walking down an alley when a shadow approached. I spotted him right away, with his hood over his eyes and his hands tucked into his pockets. It barely came as a surprise when he stopped in front of us, aiming a blade at us with shaky hands.

"Money. Jewelry. Now."

Amicia gasped, and I pushed her behind me. "Do you know who you're dealing with here?"

"Don't give a flyin' fuck," the figure snarled. He wasn't older than eighteen, still a boy. I could take him down easily. "Money. Jewels. I said fuckin' now!"

I took a step forward, sliding his hood off and exposing a young, terrified face. He glared at me, swishing the knife in my direction before he realized who I was.

"Mr... Mr. Kline," he huffed. "I'm so sorry, I had n-no idea..."

"I can see that, yes," I hissed at him. "Report to your superior, kid. You shouldn't be working in this corner."

"Y-Yes, Sir," he managed, so afraid he tumbled over his own

feet to get away. He took off running, and I sighed deeply, rubbing my eyes.

"What on earth just happened?" Amicia spoke up from behind me. "Are you okay, Sir? Did y-you know h-him?"

"Well," I started with a heavy sigh. "He knew me, and that's all you need to know right now, Kitty. Come on, it's time we went back home."

Her brows knitted together in confusion, but she didn't argue, allowing me to link our arms and pull her toward the limousine waiting a few blocks down.

I needed Kai back in town. Business was going to hell without him present, and now a street urchin had nearly harmed my Kitty. Everything was messed up.

Amicia seemed to sense my mood and remained quiet until we arrived back at home. I took her upstairs, my mind now firmly on her punishment. She hadn't forgotten about it either.

"Would you like me to prepare for..." she started, swallowing thickly. "For the punishment? Meet you in the... *room* later?"

"No," I said firmly. "Come with me now."

She followed meekly behind as I took her to the room. I dimmed the lights and ordered her to strip. She started moving her body, removing her clothes rhythmically, but I stopped her in her tracks.

"No, not like that," I said firmly. "Be quick and efficient. I want all your clothes off. Now."

She nodded, all the color draining from her face. It truly made me wonder how she'd been treated before me. I wasn't going to harm her the way she thought. I wasn't a vicious man. I wouldn't have wanted to see my marks on her for longer than a few days.

"Get up on this." I pointed to the spanking bench, and she paled, getting in position. She lay on her front, her feet on the floor and her ass exposed. "I'm going to spank you. Twenty hits. I don't want a word out of you except for 'thank you, Sir', and the numbers as you count down. Understood?"

"Yes, Sir," she whispered as I got into position behind her. "Thank you, Sir."

I got ready to start, and she shivered on the bench beneath me. I reached down to turn on the bench then, and my plaything gasped in surprise as the vibrations started kicking in.

"No coming," I told her. "No matter how good it feels. Understood?"

"Yes, S-S-Sir," she stuttered, bracing herself against the leather of the bench as the vibrations massaged her needy pussy.

I hit her for the first time, the slap reverberating through her body. "Count," I reminded her.

"Twenty."

She was trembling, but as she began counting down, those shivers turned from terrified shakiness to needy trembles that told me just how turned on she was.

I wasn't much better off. Every time my palm landed against her ass, I felt my cock painfully throb in my slacks, eager to be buried inside her. We were on day twelve and I still hadn't fucked her. Halfway done, and my cock hadn't even felt her sweet cunt yet. I wasn't sure why I was prolonging the inevitable, but it only made the prospect of her needy pussy sweeter.

"One," she finally breathed as I hit her the last time. Her worn-out body was slack against the bench, and she started to cry as I guided her off the furniture and into my arms. I knew it wasn't the pain, but instead the sweet relief of letting go.

I guided her to the bed, gently tucking her into the sheets. Her hand grabbed mine, and our eyes met, a silent war raging between us.

"Stay with me, Sir," she begged.

"I can't fuck you," I reminded her. "You'll be in too much

pain."

"Okay," she whispered. "Just stay next to me..."

I hesitated, knowing exactly what I wanted and how wrong it would be to give in to a submissive's demands. Yet I gave her a curt nod, stripped my clothes, and climbed into bed next to her.

Amicia fell asleep in my arms, and I held her close, listening to her heartbeat until we both fell into a deep, dreamless sleep.

CHAPTER 13

Amicia

Waking up in Grayson's arms felt magical. I burrowed deeper into his embrace, and he held onto me tightly, his hands embracing me and pulling me against him. My eyes fluttered open and closed slowly until they finally focused on the window. I jumped to my feet, stirring Grayson in his sleep as I pressed my palms against the glass.

"What's going on?" he spoke up sleepily from the bed as I stared outside.

"It's snowing!"

He groaned, picking himself up from the bed and joining me

by the window in nothing but boxers. "So it is. And why are you so excited about that, Kitty?"

"It's magical," I whispered, giving him a devious look. "Wouldn't you agree, Sir?"

He chuckled, pressing a kiss against my forehead. "Magical it is. Whatever you say, Kitty."

I shrieked as he grabbed for me, throwing me over his shoulder while I giggled and carrying me back to the bed we'd shared. He lay me down on my back, kissing a line down my body and making me whimper in delight. Our argument was long forgotten, all that was left of it the tension we refused to acknowledge.

Grayson raised his head, his eyes meeting mine as he gently pulled back. Frustration gripped me tightly, and I sighed out loud.

"What?" he demanded. "Wasn't that the perfect night's sleep?"

I sat up straight, my eyes boring into his as I muttered, "But I didn't want to sleep, Sir."

"No?" He cocked his head at me, an amused smile playing on his lips. "What did you want then, Kitty?"

"I wanted *you*," I whispered.

His eyes were dark and filled with naughty promises as he advanced on me, caging my body beneath his on the bed. "Is that so?"

"Yes," I managed. "I always wanted you."

"You should have told me."

"You were busy punishing me, remember?" I teased him.

"You deserved it. Naughty little thing. Tell me how you want me again."

"I want... you," I whispered, and in moments, his warm mouth covered mine. He kissed me deeply, not like an object or a plaything, but like a person he cared for. I allowed myself to live the fantasy, returning his passionate kisses as his hands ran down the length of my body, caressing inch after inch of me.

His touch turned fiery. I knew he wanted me. His hardness was pressing against me as he deepened our kiss, demanding more and more from my quivering lips. I was still naked, the only thing separating us, the thin fabric of his briefs. Finally, he pulled them down, his cock touching my bare skin for the very first time and making me gasp, eager for him to do so much more to me.

"Tell me you want this," he demanded, gripping his cock in his fist, and touching his tip to my belly. "Tell me how much you want my cock inside you, Kitty."

"I need it, Sir," I managed. "I can't be without it anymore..."

"How badly do you need it?"

"I don't think I can stand another minute without it," I groaned, twisting, and turning beneath him. "Please, Sir... Put it inside me, don't torture me anymore..."

But he wasn't done just yet. He grabbed my arms by the wrists, locking them above my head as he toyed with his dick, pressing it between my pussy lips. He was leaking precum in moments, getting me even wetter as I begged and begged for him to take mercy on me. The cruelty he'd shown me the previous night had melted away to reveal a kind, caring man who wanted to please me as much as he wanted to torture me. I was so eager for him, so ready for him to take anything he'd ever wanted from my willing body. And he knew it too, eliciting moan after moan from my parted lips.

"You're impossible to resist, Kitty," he muttered against my mouth. "Im-fucking-possible."

I hadn't heard him curse before, and the dirty word made me arch my back, ready to beg for him to take me. I didn't need to though.

His cock buried in my silky depths and I cried out with relief as he started moving in me. His hips were powerful and unrelenting, driving his cock into me again and again until stars exploded in front of my vision. He showed me pleasure in a matter of seconds, the kind I'd spent my whole life searching for. I knew the question to his answer from the previous night now more than ever.

Have you ever been in love before?

No, I have not.

Not then.

Not before *you.*

My lips parted to get the words out, but he drowned them with another demanding kiss. Grayson Kline was a passionate lover who wasn't afraid of taking what he wanted. His touch was as punishing as it was kind, and he brought me to the edge several times, pulling back just before I could come. He laughed at me, and I knew he was playing one of his endless games again as he drove into me again and again.

"Please," I rasped pleadingly. "I want to come, Sir..."

"You will," he promised me. "As soon as you tell me what you were just thinking about."

My cheeks darkened and flushed. The man was a mind reader on top of everything else. It felt like he was in my head, turning over every stone to find the truth that I'd selfishly tried to keep to myself. It was too soon... *much* too soon to admit the depth of my feelings, especially knowing he didn't feel the same way.

"I don't want to," I whispered, prompting him to reach up, brushing hair out of my face and gently wrapping his fingers around my neck. I gasped, eager for him to squeeze tighter yet too afraid to ask for the pain I hadn't known I'd been craving.

"You don't want to?" he repeated gently, and I shook my head. "I want you to though, Kitty. And that's all that matters, isn't it? That you please me."

I found myself nodding despite not wanting to admit it, and he smiled at me affectionately, groaning as my pussy clenched around his cock.

"As soon as you tell me, I'll let you come," he grunted. "An orgasm for your thoughts, my pretty Kitty..."

I didn't want to, but he'd brought me close enough to the edge that I was unable to resist, my body quivering beneath his and demanding the release he refused to give me.

"I... I have feelings for you," I blurted. "You asked me if I'd been in love... No, I haven't been."

He stilled on top of me, his eyes questioning me and his cock throbbing inside me, making me shake. "Don't lie to me, Kitty. You're not allowed to lie to me."

"I'm not," I whispered. "I'm not lying... I haven't loved anyone... not until..."

"Not until what?" His fingers tightened around my neck and I whimpered in delight.

"Not until *you*," I finished softly.

A split second later, he began fucking me again, his eyes on mine as I gasped and gasped and he brought me so close I couldn't stop saying please. Finally, he allowed it, giving me a nod, and making my eyes flutter closed as I came apart beneath him. His fingers touched the hollow in my throat, gently but firm as they pressed down on my throat, giving me an orgasm I wouldn't forget for the rest of my life.

But he wasn't done yet, and as I came down from my high, he made that clear. He drove into me again and again, giving me pleasure like I hadn't known existed. His body pumped into mine and he groaned, making sure I knew just how much I was pleasing him.

"Please, Sir," I managed. "I want to make you come, too..."

"Are you on protection?" he grunted, his eyes searching mine for the truth.

I swallowed; eyes locked with his as I shook my head.

"Fuck," he muttered, making my skin erupt in goosebumps. "I shouldn't..."

"Please." I grabbed his wrist, my eyes begging him to go on, do the unthinkable. "I don't care, just do it."

He groaned, driving himself deeper into me. He was like a man possessed, his mouth swallowing me up as he moved his hips in and out of me at a pace that made me keep coming, again and again and again.

I knew he was close, his cock throbbing inside me and leaking with wetness when he pulled back, locking eyes with me.

"You'll be the death of me, Amicia," he muttered, and I lifted my head, kissing him with every emotion he'd made me feel for the first time.

He came inside me, with my lips on his and his tongue touching mine. I gasped, and he breathed my name as he buried his cock deep within me, leaking his come out of the tip and filling me up to the very brim.

He kept rocking his hips back and forward at a steady pace, ripping one last orgasm from my worn-out body. He didn't pull out, not even when his cock stopped leaking. Instead, he pulled me into his arms and kept his cock buried deep within me.

Everything—our arguments, his work, the auction—was forgotten. The only thing that mattered was that we were together. Because together, we were perfect.

CHAPTER 14

Grayson

My eyes drank in Amicia's figure as we enjoyed our dinner together. Most nights ended like this, with us peacefully enjoying our food and retreating to my bedroom together. But that night, I had something special planned. Something that would make me very happy, and Amicia very desperate.

"Meet me in the playroom in an hour," I told her as she put her napkin down. An excited flush colored her cheeks a pretty red, like a Christmas bauble. "I have something fun planned for you tonight."

"Should I be afraid?"

"Yes," I grinned. "Very afraid indeed."

She didn't say another word, but her eyes were aglow with anticipation. I retreated to my office to finish up some work, and an hour later, walked into the playroom where she was already patiently waiting. Amicia sat on the foot of the bed, respectfully lowering her gaze when I entered the room.

"I have a special outfit for you tonight," I told her, giving her a box wrapped with a bow. "Put it on and make me a drink."

She uncovered the lid of the box. Inside was a silk red ribbon—a body bow to decorate her perfect figure, along with a pair of tall black heels. Amicia smiled and I gave her some privacy to change, admiring the London skyline through the window. It was certainly becoming colder and colder, and Christmas was approaching too fast for my liking because I knew what it meant. Losing her. And I couldn't lose her just yet. Not until I had my fill.

"Sir?"

I turned around, smiling as I saw her in front of me with a drink. I took the tumbler from her fingers, sitting down on an armchair in the room and motioning for her to come closer. Then, I finally allowed myself to drink her in.

The body bow made her look like a perfectly wrapped Christmas present. She was stunning, from the lustrous shine of her dark mane to the perfectly manicured talons. My cock tightened in my pants in anticipation, knowing I wouldn't be able to keep my hands off Amicia for much longer.

"Do you like it?" she asked, twirling in front of me. "I think it makes me look good..."

"Me too," I said gravelly, drinking a long sip of the White Russian she'd become such an expert in mixing for me. "You look sinfully good, Kitty. Do you know what we're going to do today?"

"You'll make me dance for you again?"

I shook my head, setting the now empty drink down and

motioning for her to follow me. I led her to the area of the playroom where a dark velvet curtain separated the main room from the more intense part of the area. I had kept it hidden for a while, knowing it would scare Amicia when she first arrived, but now, I knew she was ready.

A long, thin cotton rope stretched across the length of the room, with several knots placed strategically along it. Amicia was too busy fearfully looking at the crops, whips and paddles to notice it, so I gently guided her to the rope, reaching between her legs. She gasped as my fingers wrapped around the ribbon decorating her waxed pussy. I moved it to the side so her center was exposed.

"We're going to try some rope walking today," I told her with a firm smirk. "I think you'll enjoy it."

"What if I fall?"

"Not that kind of rope walking," I chuckled. She gasped as I lifted her off the floor, gently positioning her above the rope. Her gasp soon turned into a moan as I positioned her right over the first knot in the rope which was rubbing against her pussy, reminding her how much she suddenly needed stimulation.

"Sir, I..."

"It's okay." I pressed a gentle kiss against her lips. With the click of my fingers, I turned on some slow and sensual music on the speakers, and retreated to the other end of the rope. "You'll start walking soon. Go as slow as you can. If you hurry, I'll punish you."

"But..."

"But what?"

"It's... it's... frustrating," she huffed, bringing a smile to my lips. "It's making me so needy... so wet..."

"That's exactly the point, Kitty." I motioned for her to come closer. "Start walking while I pick something to punish you with."

Her eyes fearfully followed my motions as I turned to the wall, trying to pick something to hurt her with. I didn't want the whip, but I did want a cane. I picked one off the wall, thin and painful when it made contact with skin. I had never used it before.

When I turned to face Amicia, I realized she hadn't moved an inch from her position, shivering on the spot.

"Didn't you hear me?" I furrowed my brows. "Don't make me punish you for being too slow."

"Please, I-"

The cane snapped against her thigh and she yelped. A red, raw mark appeared where I hit her and she whimpered. I was turned on and almost as desperate as she was for me to be inside her. But there was an important difference between Amicia and me—I knew how to control myself, and she didn't.

"Better start walking," I reminded her. "Don't want to get hurt again, do you?"

She looked miserable as she shook her head, but we both knew that would change soon enough. She started moving then, slowly putting one foot in front of the other and coming toward me shakily.

She let out another moan as the rope dug into her skin, teasing her pussy with insufferable friction. I couldn't wait to see the wet traces of her arousal on that rope. My skin bristled with the possibilities of everything I could do to her that night.

"Come on, Kitty," I encouraged her softly. "Keep going."

"No." She shook her head, vehement. "I don't want to. It's too much."

"Did I give you a choice? It wasn't a question," I reminded her. "You signed a contract, remember?"

She just stared back stubbornly, refusing to budge from her position and just glaring at me.

"Remember your friend Capri?" I asked, eyes twinkling

darkly. "Remember who she ended up with? Don't you know how lucky you are, Amicia? I could be treating you so much worse... And you'd probably end up loving that, too."

"How dare you," she hissed.

"Watch that mouth." I hit her with the cane again and she shrieked, staring me down, obviously offended. "It will get you in too much trouble. Just be a good girl and keep walking."

"I hate you," she muttered, but along she moved, more and more moans tearing themselves from her lips as she attempted to walk closer to me.

"It's frustrating, isn't it?" I teased her mercilessly. "I bet you're getting so fucking desperate... The rope must be soaked from how dripping wet you are."

She didn't need to tell me she hated me this time—her eyes spoke for themselves. But she kept moving, and I found myself being proud of her as she kept going despite the difficulties. Her cheeks reddened into a dark red color and she looked angry, but she walked. She walked until she finally reached me, collapsing into my arms with a sob while the rope still rubbed her raw, drippy pussy.

"Good girl," I muttered into her hair. "Such a good girl. I'm so proud of you, Kitty."

Gently, I lifted her off the rope. I carried her over to the bed, but when I attempted to climb on it with her, she pushed me away. I was taken aback by her insolence, glaring down at her.

"Are you trying to get yourself punished?" She didn't answer, just stared back with pure hatred. "Ten hits with the cane. You'll count them out loud."

"Fine," she hissed, positioning herself on her belly and exposing her toned ass. "Do it if you must."

I didn't like the sudden bratty streak she'd seemed to develop, but I was certain ten hits with the cane would beat it right out of her. I started hitting her and she counted with gritted teeth. She didn't cry. She didn't beg me to stop. But when we were done, pure anger radiated from her body like warmth.

"Still hate me?" I asked her. No answer, again. "Kitty. You need to speak to me. Don't forget about the money."

"How could I?" she asked. Obviously I'd struck a nerve. "You bring it up all the time. And if this is all about the money to you, well, then-"

"Who said it was all about money to me?"

"I..." She kept glaring at me, still angry. "I know you-"

"No, you don't know anything," I interrupted. "You just think. But you don't have to think anymore. In fact, I'll make it really easy for you. Get on your back."

"But it will hurt and-"

"Get. On. Your. Back."

Teeth digging into her bottom lip, she considered her options. Soon enough, she turned around, wincing when she lay on her front. I applied salve to the marks I left on her then, carefully rubbing the red spots where the cane had hit her.

"Is that better? Can you tell I care now?" I asked.

She turned to look at me over her shoulder. "You haven't even fucked me."

"In your world, fucking means I care?" I chuckled. "I'll fuck you, Kitty. If that's what you really want."

She swallowed thickly, eyes drinking me in. Finally, she nodded without saying another word. I smirked at her.

"I should have known."

I stripped the bow off her body and she shivered beneath my touch, raw nerve endings fraying at the thought of me being inside her. But I took my time, torturing her more and more with each second that passed and I didn't give her what she was so desperate for.

"Beg me," I finally told her, fingers tracing her lips. "Beg to be fucked."

She looked like she was going to snap back, but the desperation must've gotten the best of her, and her bottom lip trembled as she said, "Please, Sir. I need you. Fuck me... Please, please, fuck me."

I took my cock out of my pants, gliding it along the red lines left on her juicy little ass. "I might pick a different hole tonight."

She gasped as she felt me poking between her cheeks. "Sir, I..."

"You don't want it?"

She swallowed thickly, eyes fearfully meeting mine. "I do... I think..."

"Good." I smirked, turning my attention to her tight ass and parting her cheeks with a groan. "Goddamn it, Kitty, you're fucking perfect."

I spat on her exposed, puckered hole, watching my spit dribble into her ass. I kept going until she was wet enough to handle me, and then started pushing inside her, gently but insistently. She gasped, and it felt like the gasp never stopped. It turned into a long, scared moan as I entered her. She was impossibly tight, making me clench my teeth together in an effort to hold back.

It would've been so easy to just fill her then and there, but I needed to pace myself, to wait before I took her fully. So I waited, slowly filling her, inch by fucking inch until she was devastatingly close, begging me for a release I was reluctant to give her since she'd been such a bad girl for me.

But as I fucked her, I found myself getting closer and closer too, and I couldn't hold back much longer, needing my Kitty as desperately as she needed me.

"You want to be filled up?" I muttered in her ear.

"Yes," she whispered. "Fill my hole, Sir..."

"Which hole?"

"My..." She swallowed thickly. "Fill my ass please, Sir."

I grabbed her hair and held it firmly in my fist as I fucked my first load into her tight, accepting hoel. She came with me, without permission, but for once, I didn't give a damn. All I wanted was to feel her body trembling against mine as I emptied my load into her.

Afterward, I held her in my arms and we fell asleep right there, in the playroom bed. I woke up sometime in the middle of the night to find her curled up practically on top of me, clinging on for dear life.

Absent-mindedly, I stroked her soft hair, wondering how this would all end.

Kitty deserved a happy ending.

CHAPTER 15

Amicia

Time was passing fast. Too fast.

We were getting closer and closer to Christmas and the date Grayson would let me go. Since I'd confessed my feelings to him, he'd been even more gentle and kind with me, but it filled me with worry that he'd send me away once our time together was up. After all, he'd paid for my time for a reason, and he'd told me plenty of times before he never kept his playthings for longer than a few weeks.

Still, I found myself hoping I'd mean more to him than most of his other toys. I wanted to stay. I wanted him to make me stay with him, to ask me to be his forever. But I hadn't expressed those thoughts yet, and as the twentieth of the month rolled around, I woke up in a cold sweat from yet another nightmare, clinging onto Grayson out of pure fear of him abandoning me.

I'd been dreaming of Margaret every night. The terrors never went away, the horrible feeling of guilt threatening to eat me up whole.

It was my fault Margaret was gone, and I'd never be able to forgive myself.

One night, years ago, I'd arranged to meet a man who'd lend me money in secret.

I hadn't wanted Margaret to find out about my secret appointment, knowing she wouldn't approve. So, I'd found the contact through a friend of a friend—someone who I knew was sketchy but could surely help me out of the hole I'd dug for myself. Loyalty bonded me to Margaret, but I was eager for dance lessons. And while I paid for her expensive groceries—none of which I ever got to experience—I kept wishing she'd lend me some money, at least a little bit, to pay for the dancing lessons I wanted to attend so very badly. But that time never came.

The man I was meeting arrived twenty minutes late, and by the time he'd appeared in the back alley behind a grocery store, I was freezing in the chilly winter air. He asked me for a name, and I instantly panicked, rattling off Margaret's name in a frenzy. The man didn't question me. He barely even looked at me, pulling out a stack of cash.

"You want this?" he'd asked me. "I've got five grand here."

"I... I don't need five grand," I'd whispered. "Just a couple hundred... I don't need much more..."

"We don't do small business like that," he'd told me. "Five grand, thirty percent interest rate. You pay us back in two months. We got a deal or not?"

I hesitated. On one hand, the money was all I'd need to get my career off the ground. I could even leave Margaret, finally be free once I turned eighteen in a few months. I found myself nodding to the man's question, and he shoved the money in my hands. I rattled off Margaret's address when he asked, then quickly pocketed the cash, and by the time I'd looked up to ask him how he'd collect the money, he'd already disappeared into the shadows.

I returned home a shaky, nervous mess. Margaret glared at me from her position in front of the TV.

"Where were you?" she'd barked at me. "I've been waiting."

"I got held up at the grocery store," I muttered, unloading the groceries on the dining table.

"Did you get it all?"

"Everything you wanted." I stored away chocolate bars and candy, steaks, expensive booze. None of it was for me. Though I cooked and prepared the food for Margaret, I existed on a diet of cheap TV dinners and ready-made meals. "I'll be in my room."

My room was a cabinet with a small bed and a chest of drawers under the stairs. I buried my hands in my coat and made a beeline for it, but Margaret stopped me with her walking stick held up in the air.

"Where are you going in that coat?" she demanded. "Take it off and hang it by the door, lazy girl."

"I..." I swallowed thickly. "I was just going to clean it."

"Looks fine to me," she barked. "And you need to get started on my ironing, anyway. Take it off."

Hesitantly, I pulled the coat off me and went to hang it by the front door. I discreetly pulled out the money and attempted to put it in my pocket, but Margaret appeared behind me, nearly scaring me to death.

"What's that?" she demanded, pulling the stack of bills out of my hands. Her eyes sparkled when she saw the money. "That's a lot of money, Amicia. Where'd a lazy girl like you get this much? Have you been whoring yourself out?"

"No," I said firmly. "I... Well, I borrowed it. I wanted to start taking dancing lessons, like I told you about."

"Dancing lessons?" she repeated, shaking her head in dismissal. "What a stupid idea. You don't need dancing lessons."

"Please, Margaret." I was reduced to begging already. "It's all I've ever wanted. I'll return the rest. I just need a couple hundred..."

"Nonsense." She smacked my hand away when I reached for the cash. "I'm keeping this. Let it serve as a lesson for you, for trying to hide this from me."

"But I have to return it!" I called out desperately. "With interest."

"I'm sure you had a plan to return it," Margaret waved her hand dismissively.

Yes, I thought to myself bitterly. *With the money I'd make once I finally got a dancing role.*

I tried to argue with her that whole night, but she'd had enough of me an hour into the conversation, beating me with her walking stick until I had to drag myself to the little room beneath the stairs. I was black and blue the next day, but that wasn't even the worst of it. Worst of all, I had to return the money Margaret had stolen from me. I wanted to cry. I wanted to beg someone for help, but where the hell was I supposed to go? There was nobody willing to help me.

The money disappeared within weeks. No dance lessons, and nothing to show for it. I knew the collector would be coming, and I was terrified.

Sure enough, two months later, the man came to collect.

He was nice enough at first, but the moment he realized I

didn't have the cash, his attitude took a turn for the worse. He told me my interest rate was now forty percent, and that he'd be back in four months.

This repeated itself until I was up to a hundred and twenty percent interest years later. I had no way of paying him, no way of getting out of the mess. I'd avoided our last few meetings, hiding from him, because I didn't have any money to give him. By then, I'd picked up a job at a seedy bar waitressing. I hated it, but I painstakingly put every pound Margaret begrudgingly allowed me to keep aside. Still, I didn't have much. Certainly not enough to cover my growing debt.

I was plagued with worry, constantly thinking about the money I owed. I was making my way home from a long shift at the bar, barely able to think about everything else I still had to do when I came home to a door that had been left open.

The apartment was dark. I couldn't hear the usual blare of the TV, and the fact that the door was open was strange. Margaret never went anywhere. I knew instantly something was wrong.

"Margaret?" I called out, carefully opening the door.

No answer.

I turned on the hallway light and gasped when I saw the mess I'd walked into.

The apartment had been ransacked. My things and Margaret's possession lay everywhere, littering the floor. Someone had turned it upside down.

I rushed inside and started screaming the moment I walked into the living room. Margaret was there, in front of the turned-off TV. Her unseeing eyes were staring at nothing, mouth hanging wide open in a silent scream. There was blood everywhere. She'd been shot in the chest.

The rest of it was a blur. I called the police. They tried to accuse me at first, but I had an alibi—the bar job. The intruder had taken anything of value. The money I'd hid, Margaret's jewelry, everything.

They asked me whether I had any idea of who could've done it, and I'd shook my head no. The shame of it all still burned me every time I thought back to that time. It was my fault they killed her. I'd given the man Margaret's name, and now she was gone, and the debt was, in their mind, paid off.

But that wasn't the end of the story.

The apartment I'd been counting on was rented, and the moment the landlord found out what happened, he kicked me out. I spent four nights on the streets before I found a new place. I started dancing at *Le Cabaret*. Then, the banks came.

In her fifty-eight years, Margaret had racked up an impressive debt with every bank in London. Altogether, she owed over ten thousand pounds. She'd co-signed my name on every one of the loans she'd taken. Nobody believed me when I told them she'd forged my signature. I was the only one left—she'd had no family, and the banks needed someone who'd pay.

So, my new life began. Paying off the loans one by one while dancing at *Le Cabaret*, trying desperately to pursue my dream which seemed further and further out of reach.

Everything changed when I found out about the auction.

Everything changed when I met *him*.

As he held me after my nightmare, I wondered whether my luck had finally turned. Maybe Grayson would take care of me. Maybe I'd finally be allowed to dance.

"It's okay," he whispered against my hair. "You're okay, my darling. You're going to be fine."

I burrowed deeper into his embrace, relishing the feeling of being close to him. I wanted so much more—to belong to him, to be his like no other plaything had been before. But he still hadn't revealed the depth of his own feelings for me.

"Can we spend today together?" I whispered.

He pondered my words, then his face broke into a smile. "Of course, Kitty. I'm taking the last few days with you off. You're all mine until Christmas... and I'm all yours."

I was too scared to ask what would happen after that.

***

"We're going to do something fun tonight," Grayson told me over dinner, and I smiled at him.

"Oh?"

"You'll like it," he promised with a devious smile.

"If you say so, I believe you, Sir."

He squeezed my hand beneath the table, and I beamed at him before returning to my food. Butterflies were fluttering in my stomach, more and more every time I was near Grayson. I had been falling for him from the beginning, but now... Now I was foolishly, hopelessly, and desperately in love with the man who'd paid hundreds of thousands to own me for twenty-four days.

After dinner, we relaxed in front of the fireplace together. I sat by Grayson's feet, and he absent-mindedly threaded his fingers through my hair as he went through some paperwork. When the clock struck ten o'clock, he put his phone away and pulled me to my feet.

"The room," he said. "In ten minutes. I want you naked on the bed, Kitty. Understood?"

"Yes, Sir." His order sent a shiver down my spine.

I got ready for him. I'd been waxed the day before, and the exercise routine he kept me on had transformed my body from the malnourished, skinny thing it had been before into a perfectly toned figure. I was more confident than I'd ever been before, and I lived for Grayson's appreciative gaze sliding over my body as he drank me in.

I kept my promise, meeting him in the secret room after ten minutes had passed. I sat on the bed, naked and waiting for him, my breath catching in my throat as he entered the room.

I felt shivers go down my spine as Grayson's figure appeared in the doorway. He stood there, illuminated by the dimmed lights and making my heart race faster than ever. He was carrying a box, and he turned to close the door before bringing it over to the bed.

I sat on my knees, my eyes drinking him in as he opened the box. I didn't dare look inside, instead focusing my gaze on him.

"Am I being punished?" I whispered.

"No, Kitty," he replied firmly. "Far from it. You're being rewarded."

"What for?"

"For being the best plaything, I could possibly wish for," he told me tenderly, his fingers caressing my cheek before he motioned to the box. "Don't you want to see what I have for you?"

I crawled closer, sneaking a peek into the box. It was filled with Christmas lights.

"What's this?" I laughed. "Are we decorating another tree?"

"No, my pretty Kitty," he said affectionately, chuckling. "We're decorating *you*."

He ordered me to lie on my back, taking out string after string of Christmas lights while ambient Christmas music played in the background. Slowly, he began wrapping me in the Christmas lights. He tied up my ankles together before moving onto my wrists. He tied me firmly, but not too tightly to make it uncomfortable. Somehow, the fact that I was now unable to move turned me on. I was at his mercy… and a part of me *hoped* he'd be rough with me.

Grayson turned on the Christmas lights, illuminating my body with pretty colorful lights. I laughed, feeling excited like I hadn't ever before. Christmas was just another day in my life, but here, with Grayson, it had turned into a special occasion worth celebrating.

He took special time and care to touch every inch of me, explaining the lights wouldn't burn my skin and I need only tell him if I felt uncomfortable. But I assured him I was comfortable—even excited—about being tied up for him. I relished the feeling of him taking control over me. I wanted him to do so much more.

Grayson explored my body with his fingers first and his tongue second. He sucked on my nipples, making them pebble in his mouth before moving between my legs, making me moan helplessly as he continued his gentle assault. I melted beneath his touch, ready for so much more, but he kept the balance perfect—a mix of pleasure from being touched and trepidation from being tied up and at his mercy.

He brought me to two orgasms before he even took his cock out. And when he did, I was ready, wet and willing at the sight of him and eager for him to fuck me. He took his precious time, edging me for what felt like hours before allowing me another orgasm.

"Please, Sir," I begged him. "I want your cock inside me…"

"Are you going to let me use protection this time, Kitty?" Grayson chuckled softly.

I locked eyes with his, biting my lower lip as I shook my head no. His expression darkened, and the need to have me took over. He positioned me on my knees then, putting his cock inside me as I gasped for more. It was even more special, almost dangerous because of the way he tied me up, but it only served to make me more excited.

He fucked me relentlessly that night, but after his first orgasm, he didn't stop. He kept going, but it was no longer fucking—no, this was making love, pure and simple. He treated me like a priceless object, a goddess sent to Earth for his own pleasure. I'd never felt as cherished as I did in his arms, with his eyes locked on mine and our bodies moving together, seeking an orgasm that rocked through us at the same time.

After he was done, depositing his second load of the night deep within me, he finally undid the Christmas lights strung around my limbs and held my shaking, recovering body in his arms, kissing me all over. I started giggling then, and the sweet sound of his laughter followed suit. He cupped my face, kissing me deeply and never taking his eyes off mine.

"Kitty," he spoke up. "Are you happy here, with me?"

"Yes, Sir," I whispered. "Do you…"

"Do I what?" he spoke after I paused. "Ask me, Kitty."

"Do you…" I swallowed the lump in my throat. "Do you want to keep me, Sir?"

He smiled at me affectionately, his eyes filled with dark promises as he nodded. "Of course, I do, Amicia. I've wanted to keep you since the moment I laid eyes on you."

I breathed a sigh of relief as he kissed me again, muttering against my lips, "But you know what that means, don't you, Kitty?"

"What?"

"We can't have secrets from one another," he said gently. "So after your time is over… I want you to tell me everything. Every little thing about you."

I swallowed again, my eyes darkening with worry.

"I see the fear inside you," Grayson told me. "I can see your brain working, the cogs turning. You can't get away from me, Kitty. I'm going to know every thought in your head. Is that okay with you?"

"Yes, Sir," I whispered.

"Good Kitty," he muttered before pulling me firmly against

him. "Now let's sleep together. The time for secrets will come."

He fell asleep moments after that, but I lay awake in his arms for hours after our conversation.

Grayson was right. I needed to tell him the truth. About Margaret, the loan shark, and the debt I'd inherited. He deserved to know everything about me.

Even if it meant we couldn't be together.

CHAPTER 16

Grayson

It was Kitty's last day. She would be allowed to leave after the clock struck midnight and the twenty-fourth of December became the twenty-fifth.

I was developing feelings for my Kitty, but what worried me more than knowing it myself was the thought of her finding out. Somehow, I was convinced I'd show her a weaker side of me if she found out about my growing crush. It wasn't even a crush anymore. No, it was full-blown...

I shook my head to get the thought out. I couldn't think about that now, not with the date she was supposed to leave me fast approaching. I'd known from the start I wouldn't be able to keep her forever, but now, knowing how soon she'd leave me, I was at the same time eager for her to stay and wanting to keep my true feelings hidden. It was a way of protecting myself. If she didn't know how much she meant to me already, she wouldn't know how much she'd hurt me by leaving. And if she did, she could use it as a weapon against me.

It was Christmas Eve and we sat down to dinner in front of the luxuriously decorated tree. I'd had a chef flown in to cook for us that night, and we sat through course after incredible course accompanied by some of the best wine money could get. Kitty was getting tipsy, throwing her head back in laughter, her eyes glittering as she drank her wine. It was a perfect night. In my mind, nothing could go wrong—that is, until a phone call interrupted me.

I took a quick look at the screen, muttering an apology to my tipsy plaything as I answered the call. "Hello?"

"Boss, it's me."

"Kai," I said with a smile. "About time you called. Can I take this to mean you're officially back in London?"

"I am, Sir," he went on, the sound of traffic heavy behind him. "I'll drop by the penthouse tonight, Sir, bring over a few things you'll need. It's just paperwork but I'll need your signature on it right away."

"Of course, Kai," I went on, glancing at Amicia. "But we'll have to hurry it along. I'm in the company of a beautiful woman and I don't want to waste time on business."

Amicia grinned widely at me and I cut the call after agreeing Kai would drop by in the next twenty minutes. For the rest of the evening, I teased Kitty about the presents I'd gotten her. There seemed to be a consensus in the room that she'd still be there when I woke up in the morning. But I knew as well as she did, she'd be free to leave after midnight. Though I wasn't certain I could just let her walk away.

Minutes later, the doorbell sounded, and a waiter I'd hired for the evening let Kai in. I waited by the elevator, grinning wide when I saw my right-hand man walk through the door.

"Kai! How good to have you back. Florian isn't half as helpful as you are."

"I'm flattered, Sir," Kai replied firmly, ever the professional as he handed me a stack of papers. "Your paperwork. Shall I wait for you to sign it?"

"Yes, please. Do come in. I want to introduce you to Amicia."

"The new toy? Are you happy with her, Sir?" Kai seemed genuinely curious.

"She's the best one I've ever had," I replied with certainty. "I want to keep her. Don't tell her though. It'll go right to her head."

Kai chuckled, shaking his head. "Of course not, Sir."

I guided him into the living room where Amicia was waiting. She turned around with a brilliant smile, wearing a gorgeous silk red dress I'd picked for her and with two wine glasses in hand. But the moment she saw Kai standing next to me, the smile on her face disappeared. Her hands shook so badly she dropped both glasses. The crash of them on the floor was like a slap to the face.

"Kitty?" I questioned. "Is everything alright?"

"Sir," she spoke up shakily. "Please... Please get me away from him." She pointed to Kai with a shaky finger while he glared at her. "Don't let him come near me."

"What the hell?" I asked, looking between them. "Do you two know each other?"

"Indeed, we do," Kai hissed, pushing up the sleeves of his shirt. "What is this, some kind of con attempt?"

"No," Amicia cried out. "I didn't know... I didn't know Grayson worked for you!"

"He doesn't work for me, stupid girl," Kai interrupted with a threatening laugh. "I work for *him*."

"W-What?" Amicia's eyes turned to mine. I could tell she felt betrayed. "*You're* the one I owe money to?"

"Excuse me?" I asked.

"It's her, Sir." Kai motioned to Amicia. "She's the girl who gave us the fake name. She owes you five grand, plus enough interest to make it twenty."

My head was spinning from this information, and I glared at Amicia. "*You're* the con artist who cost me money?"

"No," she snarled in response. "You're the monster who killed my foster parent."

She took off running, and I turned to face Kai. "I need to deal with this."

"Certainly, Sir." Kai leaned in with a blank look on his face. "But this one is not to be trusted. If you need me to... *dispose* of her, just give me a sign."

I slammed him against the wall the next second. "You touch her, you die. Understood?"

"Yes, Sir." I let him go, and Kai refused to meet my eyes as he buttoned his suit. "I'll be back tomorrow for the papers."

I didn't reply as he went down in the lift. My priority was Amicia. I had no idea what had just happened, but things were slowly becoming clear—the puzzle pieces coming together in my mind.

There had only ever been one person who'd wronged me, and that had been years ago, when most of my business was still... shady, to say the least.

And it turned out that person was the woman I'd bought.

Amicia ran back into the room, marching toward the lift. She snarled when I tried to grab her.

"Where the hell do you think you're going?" I demanded.

"I'm leaving," she hissed. "I can't possibly stay after this.

How do you think I feel?"

"How do you think *I* feel?" I returned the question. "I just found out you're the one who got away with my cash. I *killed* for you, Amicia."

"No! You killed because you're a monster," she snarled at me, grabbing a steak knife from the dining table with shaky hands and aiming it at me. "Don't touch me, and don't you dare come any closer."

"Amicia," I begged her, trying to stay level-headed.

"No," she cried out. "Don't even speak to me. You had her killed! The wrong woman, Grayson! You killed her!"

"I didn't kill her," I pointed out.

"No," she shook her head. "You had someone else do your dirty work, because you're a fucking coward, Grayson Kline."

"Watch your tongue."

"No. Fuck you!"

"Watch it!" I lunged for her and she shrieked, swinging her knife. She got me in the right forearm, slashing through the fabric of my designer suit and leaving a long, bloody line on my arm. "Look what you did, Kitty. Now I'm going to have to punish you."

"You won't touch me ever again," she snarled.

"Oh, but I will." My cruel side was coming out to play, and I hated myself for it. But I had to discipline her. She knew what kind of man I was now, after all. "If you leave now, you can kiss your money goodbye. You have to stay until Christmas morning. Then, it's up to you what you want to do."

"Fuck you," Amicia said. "I can't believe you'd make me stay here with you, you sick bastard."

"The more names you call me, the harder you'll have to work to apologize," I hissed. "Now drop that knife. Drop. It. Now!"

The knife clattered from her trembling fingers, falling to the floor, and we glared at one another.

"You can force me to fuck you," Amicia said. "But I'll never forgive you for what you did, and I'll never forget who you really are, Grayson."

"I have no plans of forcing you," I clipped back. "But I'll take special care in making you beg for me to fuck you. Now get the hell over here."

She shook her head furiously, and I attempted to grab her. The girl slipped between my fingers, taking off down the hallway while I chased her. She had nowhere to go. I caught her on the balcony, her fingers gripping the fence.

"Let go of me!" she demanded. "Let go of me or I jump!"

She put one of her high-heeled legs on the fence and I took a step back, holding my hands up. "Calm down, Kitty. Don't do anything stupid."

She broke down then, sobs racking her sweet little body until she was a mess of runny makeup and disheveled hair. I tried to approach her, but she hissed at me every time I came near.

"Kitty," I spoke up again, trying to remain calm. "I'm going back inside. Come with me. Let me make it better."

I took a step back inside the penthouse, holding out a hand for her. Several excruciating seconds passed before she finally reached forward, intertwining her fingers with mine. I pulled her against me, breathing a sigh of relief when her body crashed against mine.

Moments later, I guided her back into the room, whispering sweet nothings into her ear to calm her down. She was shaking. My own guilt was eating me up, and I fucking hated it. Not because of Amicia, but because no one before her had made me feel angry at myself like this.

I was a man of business. Whether that business was shady or not was something my conscience had to work out. I'd never given a shit about the opinions of others. But not with Amicia.

With her, I wanted approval. And I knew I would never have it again—at least not from her, the one who mattered most.

I guided her into the bedroom, not the guest one where she'd slept on the first night, and not the playroom's bed, but the master bedroom where none of my female friends had ever slept before her. I removed her clothes carefully while she sobbed. I understood then that finding out what she did had broken her. I knew there'd be no going back from what she'd just discovered. She'd never forgive me.

All we had was this one last night.

And I was going to make it one to remember.

I held Amicia's trembling body in my arms that night, whispering how much she meant to me in her ear. I'd never done that for a woman, not even another human being. She made me human again. She turned the monster I'd been for the past few decades into someone with a heart.

I knew she wanted to leave. Her body was there, but her mind didn't want to be with me.

"Stay with me," I said to her. "One last night. Tomorrow you can leave. Just let me have one last night."

She didn't respond, her body rigid in my arms. I wanted her to reassure me, but I knew she wouldn't. I'd fucked up. She knew what I was now. There was no going back from this.

We lay there for hours. I kept whispering in her ear and she moved further and further away from me in the bed.

"I loved you," she whispered in the middle of the night. "And you broke me."

I could have told her I loved her too, but I was too ashamed.

So, I just listened to the sound of her sweet sobbing until sleep pulled us both under.

***

I woke up to sunshine streaming in through the window, with snowflakes dancing in the icy day. My first thought was of her, my sweet Kitty, and my arms sought her out in the bed next to me, coming up empty. She wasn't there. I should have known then she was gone, but I pretended she'd just gone to the bathroom.

I pulled myself out of bed and checked the rooms one by one. She wasn't in the secret room. Not in any of the bathrooms or the other bedrooms. She wasn't in the kitchen, the study, or the living room. The Christmas tree stood there, a silent reminder of Christmas Day—the day she was finally supposed to become mine, and the one I'd forever remember as the first one without her.

Nearing the tree, I took in gift after gift, wrapped up all pretty and waiting for Amicia to tear into the wrapping paper. Except that would never happen now. I'd given her the opportunity to leave, and she had. I had no right to my Kitty anymore, and we both knew it. I'd given that up myself.

I picked up one of the smallest packages, carefully unwrapping it myself. I revealed a dark blue velvet box, opening it to reveal a priceless engagement ring. In the cold light of the morning, the ring was tacky and too gaudy for a girl like Amicia. She deserved something more special.

I walked over to the balcony, pondering the ring in my hands. It was the sign of our relationship falling apart. Another symbol of my ownership over the girl who hadn't wanted to be owned. Taking one last, long look at the ring, I tossed it over the balcony and into the abyss below.

Walking back inside, I groaned when I saw the Christmas tree. I'd have to arrange to have it taken down—I couldn't bear the sight of it, remembering how happy we'd been putting it up together.

A package on the floor caught my attention. It wasn't one of the ones I'd had professionally wrapped, it was a simple gift box with a bow clumsily attached to the top. I picked it up, reading my name in Amicia's neat handwriting scribbled on the front. Had she left it on purpose, or had she forgotten she'd left it there?

I ripped through the paper in record time, lifting the lid of the box with a deep sigh. Inside, Kitty's mask from that first night at *Le Cabaret* was waiting, all pink sequins and cute kitty ears. I touched the fabric longingly, and every moment I'd spent with my plaything flashed in my mind, a painful reminder of how alone her absence had made me.

My fingers wrapped around the mask and I cursed softly. I couldn't let her go. Even though she'd chosen to leave me, I couldn't accept it. I wanted to keep my Kitty. I wanted to have her back.

And I knew then and there I wouldn't stop hunting her until she was finally mine again.

CHAPTER 17

Amicia

11 months later

lmost a year had passed since I left Grayson Kline's London penthouse in tears. I thought the memories would fade faster, but it seems as if the old wounds will never heal. As I walk through the streets of my favorite city in the world that day, huddling into my coat, I find myself wishing I'd never closed the door on our relationship.

Yes, it was awful what happened because of Grayson. But I'd played a role in it too, and the only person I'd blamed when I left was him, even though there was just as much guilt on my own shoulders.

The freezing cold made me shiver as I came up to my apartment building. It had been a long year with a lot of changes, most of them for the better. Now that I had more money, I could finally afford better things, including my apartment which was small, but cozy. It wasn't quite as nice as Mr. Kline's penthouse, but I was perfectly happy with it.

Still, the worst of it all was the overwhelming loneliness I felt every day. Since I'd stopped dancing at *Le Cabaret*, I hadn't kept in touch with any of my friends from back there. I didn't hear from Capri after the auction either, which made me worried. I hoped she was okay, but there wasn't much I could do for her, not anymore. Not without Grayson.

I put on the kettle and made myself a cup of tea. I had a date that night, my first since the Grayson ordeal. I had a new job at a restaurant then. The tips were good and the clientele was much better than I was used to. But I hadn't really made friends there. Still, one of the bartenders liked me enough to ask me out, and I found myself agreeing. It was the time of year when I hated being lonely. The memory of Grayson was still overwhelming, so I welcomed the distraction of a new man.

His name was Ross, and he was tall, with blonde hair and blue eyes. I liked the way his eyes crinkled when he smiled, and the dimples in his cheeks. I wasn't sure how successful our date would be, but I was excited to find out if Ross would be able to make me forget about Grayson for the night.

I got ready, putting on a simple jewel-toned purple dress with knitted tights and black heeled boots. I put on my new coat—with buttons, what a relief—and added a grey scarf. Ross and I were meeting at the restaurant which was only a block away. For some reason, I hadn't felt comfortable enough to give him my address just yet. As I walked briskly through the November cold, I found myself wondering why I was so reluctant to share with Ross.

Ross was already waiting by the time I got to the restaurant. He kissed my cheek and we smiled at one another a little awkwardly.

"So where are we going?" I asked.

"I thought here would be perfect," he grinned.

"Mario's?" I glanced at the restaurant behind us. "Oh, okay. Sure."

I was a little disappointed but I did my best not to let it show. I didn't want him to know I was stuck-up or something. But the truth was, I'd spent most of my time at *Mario's* and I was dreading spending another minute in that place. But I swallowed back my reply and followed him into the room. Our coworkers smiled and led us to an empty table in a good spot.

"Best table in town," Ross joked, and I gave him a tense smile.

He ordered the food for us without asking for my preference. I didn't argue, though I already had a feeling this date wasn't going well. For the next hour while we made our way through our appetizers and main courses, Ross talked about himself. He didn't ask me anything about myself and an hour into the date, I'd already written it off as a disaster.

My eyes wandered from Ross animatedly chatting about his pitbull in front of me, and I found myself thinking of the one person I'd tried the hardest to banish from my thoughts—Grayson Kline.

I couldn't help it. I hadn't imagined our connection—I knew he felt it, too. But in the past eleven months, Grayson had made no attempt to contact me. He'd probably moved on already. He had the wealth and resources to find a new toy, someone more agreeable than I had been.

My fingers dug into the cloth napkin on my lap. Even after all these months, it hurt to imagine him with someone else. I couldn't think about it, it made me sick.

And yet I couldn't bring myself to stop. Margaret's image appeared in my mind again. The cruel woman had shaped my life into something I barely recognized anymore. I'd spent years resenting her and more years resenting myself for what I'd done. But I needed to move on. Margaret was gone, and I deserved a new, brighter future without her in it.

"Oh god," Ross groaned in front of me, palming his suit pocket. "I think I forgot my wallet."

Great, I thought to myself. What a perfect ending to a perfect freaking day.

"That's fine," I replied coolly. I paid for our meal, resenting the whole date since I hadn't even gotten to pick what I ate. I rarely treated myself like this, despite the growing money in my bank account. I didn't want to spend carelessly.

Ross offered to walk me home and I reluctantly accepted, just because it was dark and I was worried, and certainly not because I wanted to invite him back upstairs. But judging by the shit-eating grin on his face when I said yes, that was exactly what he was expecting to happen. I groaned inwardly. I would let him down easy, despite the ungentlemanly way he'd handled our date.

As we walked, his endless tirade about himself continued. I don't know if he thought the date was going well—I certainly didn't. All I could think about was curling up in my bed and forgetting this date had ever happened. Of course, now I also had to worry about all my coworkers knowing I went out with Ross, which would be a nightmare I'd have to deal with the next day.

Suppressing a groan, I motioned to an apartment building. "This is mine."

"Great," he smirked, winking at me. "Let's go upstairs."

"Oh," I wrinkled my nose. "I'd actually like to get an early night."

"Oh come on," he laughed, leaning against the brick wall. "You're not even going to invite me upstairs after tonight?"

My patience was wearing thin, but I didn't want to be rude, so I just shrugged. "Sorry."

"You can't be serious." He furrowed his brows at me, obviously displeased. "You're really going to treat me like that? Are you telling me I wasted my Friday night on you?"

"I'm sorry," I repeated. "But let's recap tonight. You took me to my own workplace for dinner. You didn't ask me a single thing about myself. You 'forgot' your wallet. And now you're offended because I won't let you come in?"

He reddened, obviously stewing with anger. "Entitled fucking bitch."

"Yeah, thanks." I fought the urge to cry, even though my first instinct was to slap his face. "I'll see you at work, Ross."

"You're gonna walk away from this?" He blocked my path all of a sudden, and I recoiled from the smell of booze on his breath. I had noticed he'd drank most of the bottle of wine we'd had with dinner, but the stench made me think he'd drunk something before then, too. "I don't think so, bitch."

"I'm afraid that's not up to you," I muttered, trying to walk past him. But he kept blocking my way until I finally looked up, my eyes meeting his murky, enraged gaze. "Please let me go home, Ross."

"No fucking way," he snarled, droplets of spittle landing on my face from his open mouth. "You're not getting away that easily. I'm owed at least a kiss if nothing else."

"I don't owe you anything," I bit back. "Move, or I'm pushing you."

"You could try," he laughed nastily. "But I'm bigger and stronger. And you're not just going to leave me on the street with my dick hard, are you?"

Ignoring his words, I came through on my promise and attempted to push him away. But when I did, he grabbed me by the wrist and pulled me in close. His eyes looked manic and for the first time in the evening, I found myself getting scared.

"You always treat men like this, Amicia?" he barked at me. "I think it was about time someone taught you a lesson."

"Let go," I demanded, trying to pull my arm out of his grasp but failing. "I'm leaving, we're done here."

"We're done when I say we're done," he snarled. "Now give me a kiss, I've been waiting all fucking night..."

He attempted to kiss me, sloppy lips trying to find mine. Finally, I found my voice, shrieking loudly as his hands started roaming all over my unwilling body. "Let me go! Stop this! Get off!"

"Get your hands off her right the fuck now."

Both Ross and I froze when a third voice joined the chorus. I recognized that voice, and my eyes flitted behind Ross, my stomach sinking. It *was* him—Kai, Grayson's right hand man.

"Mind your own business," Ross spat out.

"Didn't I tell you to take your hands off her?" Kai insisted calmly. I heard a click then, and my date's eyes widened in fear. He raised his arms in the air.

"Calm down, would you?" he asked, nervous. "I was just walking her home."

"No you weren't," I hissed in response. "You groped me!"

"Shut the fuck up," he snarled at me. "Can't you see he's got a gun pointed at me?"

My body froze. All my memories of finding Margaret's body came flooding back. She'd been shot point-blank and left for dead. I closed my eyes, unable to deal with the situation at hand.

"You don't ever speak to her again," Kai hissed at Ross. "Tomorrow you find a new job and hand in your notice at *Mario's*.

You're fucking done. Got it?"

"I got it," Ross said, whimpering as Kai shoved the gun behind his back. "Fuck, just let me go. I won't even look at her again, I swear..."

"If you do, I'm taking your finger off that hand next time," Kai hissed. "Now get the fuck lost."

Ross scampered down the alley, breaking into a run and fearfully glancing over his shoulder as he did his best to get away from me.

"Are you okay?" Kai asked, and I nodded, refusing to meet his eyes. This man was a cold-blooded killer. I'd never be able to come to terms with that. "I'm sorry I didn't intervene sooner."

"How did you even know I was here?" I snapped, tucking a strand of hair behind my ear self-consciously. "Did he send you?"

"Mr. Kline, ah..." He smiled. "He asked me to keep an eye out for you."

"Tonight?" I demanded. By his smile, I knew that wasn't the case. "How long have you been following me around?"

"Since you left the penthouse," he finally admitted.

"That's sick," I muttered, even though I was secretly grateful. "Leave me alone."

I walked past him to the door of my building, feeling his gaze on my back as I unlocked the door.

"Miss Romano?"

I turned over my shoulder reluctantly to look at Kai. "What?"

"Mr. Kline cares about you very much," he said. "Please do try not to get hurt and avoid dubious characters like this one."

"Fine," I hissed, narrowing my eyes at him before grumbling, "And thanks. I guess."

"You're welcome, Miss Romano."

The sight of Kai's sparkling dark eyes followed me as I went upstairs to my apartment. He'd just saved me, and I had Grayson to thank for that. Despite my annoyance, I couldn't fight the tell-tale smile off my lips.

CHAPTER 18

Grayson

I had never taken my eyes off the prize. I wanted her back, and ever since she left my penthouse that crisp Christmas morning, I knew I had to get her back no matter the cost.

Despite my best intentions, I'd fallen in love with Amicia Romano. I'd tried fighting it for a long time. The weeks she spent at my penthouse apartment were spent with my eyes closed, vehemently telling myself I didn't feel what I felt. But the moment she left, she left a hole behind, and I knew no other woman could ever fill that hole again.

I had trained myself not to love. Had spent years proving to myself I didn't need anyone else to be happy. But when Amicia left, I realized that didn't matter. I could be reasonably happy without her, but it wasn't enough. I wanted her, needed her. And I wasn't giving up until she was back in my arms where she belonged.

"Mr. Kline?"

"Yes, I'm sorry." I smiled at the girl sitting in front of my desk. "My mind drifted for a moment."

"It's okay." The girl smiled nervously. "Thank you for giving me the opportunity to speak to you tonight."

"Of course," I nodded. She was always so very polite.

I liked the girl. Her name was Georgina, and she was one of the first students we'd accepted into our scholarship program. I'd invented it to commemorate Amicia, and I hoped she would be as proud as I was of our budding talents. Georgina was one of them, a talented singer from the wrong side of the tracks who'd spent her life in foster care just like the other children. I hoped that, with the help of my program, she'd be able to find success in the world of music, like she'd dreamed of her whole life.

She was a cute kid, with her red hair perpetually in pigtails with ribbons at the ends and freckles all over her upturned nose. She was eleven, but seemed wiser beyond her years. She reminded me of Amicia in a lot of ways. She had a certain kind of wisdom about her, perhaps from being let down by the system which had done nothing but pass her around.

I'd first met her a few months ago. She was the reason I started planning the scholarship program. My business was sponsoring a talent show at a local public school, and I was forced to go to the show. I dreaded going for weeks, but that stopped the moment I heard Gerogina's angelic voice. She hit every note and impressed me with her talents at such a tender age. From the moment I saw her on stage, I saw that certain je ne sais quoi Amicia had as well.

This girl was born for the stage—to perform and to be a star.

I'd inquired about Georgina after the concert, finding out she was currently living in a London orphanage and waiting to be adopted into a foster home. I took her out for ice cream and watched her with a smile on my face as she devoured the sundae I got her. She told me she'd never had a treat like that and my heart hurt for her. We never spoke about her life, but instead of my plans for the scholarship I'd created with her and Amicia in mind.

She was beyond excited, and I promised her the first spot. I stayed true to my promise, and two months later, she was granted scholarship to an expensive musical school she could never have gone to otherwise. Soon enough, other kids entered the scholarship program, too. There were dancers, singers, artists. I wanted to take care of them all, but Georgina always had a special place in my heart. It wasn't just her said life story that endeared her to me. The girl was intelligent, sweet and kind, and reminded me of a daughter Amicia and I could have had once upon a time, before I'd ruined things.

Often, I'd find myself fantasizing about a future in which Amicia, Georgina and I were together.

Soon enough, I decided to change that dream into a plan.

"Georgina, do you have another minute?" I wondered out loud, and she nodded, sitting back down. "I wanted to talk to you about something else, ah... a special woman in my life."

"Oh, Mr. Kline." She giggled. "Did you fall in love?"

"I..." My brows furrowed. I didn't want to answer her question and yet I found myself nodding, the image of the strict, powerful businessman I'd worked to build over the years shattering in front of this innocent girl. "I suppose I did, yes."

"She's one very lucky lady," Georgina smiled wide. "What did you want to talk about?"

"I wanted to organize something special for her," I said,

leaning forward on my desk. "See, I haven't seen her in a long time. Almost a year."

"That is long," she said, cocking her head to the side. "Don't you love her? She must miss you very much."

I smiled softly. "I certainly hope she does. In either case, I'm trying to plan something special for this woman, and I would love it if you could help me organize it."

"What do you need help with?" she wondered out loud. "I don't think I can do much... I don't have any money."

I chuckled. "Money's not a problem, Georgina. But what I do need is your wonderful voice."

I explained the plan to her, and by the end of it, she was clapping her hands together with excitement. "Oh, what a wonderful idea, Mr. Kline. I'm sure your friend will absolutely love that. She will be sure to forgive you."

"Forgive me?" I knitted my brows together.

"Well, you never said she was angry, but I figured you did something wrong," she said, flushing. "I'm sorry, Mr. Kline."

"It's quite alright, Georgina," I muttered. "You're right. I did do something wrong. I let her go."

***

I returned to my penthouse that night with my head swimming with thoughts. I was thinking of Amicia even more than I usually did. It was all because of that encounter Kai had described to me. I resented myself for not being there to fucking strangle the man who'd dared put his hands on my Kitty. I would've killed him, of that, I was certain.

As I jumped in the shower and the hot water sprayed over my body, I closed my eyes and found my thoughts circling around her again.

Spending last December with her was one of my most treasured memories. Sometimes, I still couldn't quite believe she was gone. I'd wake up in the morning, still foolishly trying to find her body in the bed next to me. But Amicia was gone, and unless I proved to her I was a changed man, she would never take me back.

My hand found its way between my legs. My cock was hard at the memory of her soft limbs intertwined with mine. I groaned. I couldn't get her off my mind.

At first, I'd tried. I'd convinced myself she'd never take me back, not after what I'd done to her. But I soon realized I wouldn't be able to live without her. I needed her like I needed oxygen. She was an inescapable need and I was done running away from what I really, truly, deeply wanted. And that was Amicia Romano. She was the one for me.

I heard the faint buzzing of my phone outside. Not many people had my private number, so I knew this wasn't a good sign. With a groan, I turned off the water and dried my hair. I called the number back.

"Mr. Kline?"

"Speaking."

"You were listed as an emergency contact for Miss Georgina Skye."

"Yes?" My blood ran cold at the mention of her name. "Is she okay?"

"There's been... an incident," the cool voice informed me. "Can you come to the Home? I'm afraid Miss Georgina can't stay here tonight."

"Of course."

I rushed to get ready, pulling clothes on and waking up my driver. He took me to the home where Georgina lived, and I furrowed my brows as I walked into the headmistresses' office where Georgina sat red-faced, tears drying on her young face.

"What happened here?" I barked at the headmistress, Miss Shannon. "Why is she crying?"

"Georgina tried to avoid her punishment tonight," Miss Shannon informed me in a clipped voice. "She directly disobeyed orders."

"You hit me," Georgina spat out with an accusing glare.

"Shut up, girl."

"Don't talk to her like that," I cut in sharply. "Did you hit her?"

The woman's lips set into an even thinner, unattractive line. "I did what I had to do."

"You don't hit a child," I barked at her. "Come on Georgina, we're leaving."

The woman stood up as Georgina followed me out of the room. "Just so you know, Mr. Kline. She's not welcome here anymore. Good girl finding a foster home for an insolent girl like her."

"Good luck becoming a better human," I told her. "Doesn't take a genius to work out you need some help in that department."

Georgina gathered her things and followed me into the car silently clutching her battered suitcase of meager possessions. I vowed to make things better for her then and there, but for the time being, she'd have to spend the night in the penthouse.

"Are you okay?" I asked on the drive back, and she nodded, staring out of the window. "Where did that woman hit you?"

"On my arm," she muttered.

"Does it hurt?" She just shrugged. "You can stay with me tonight. Then we'll work on finding you a foster home as soon as possible. You have an aunt, right?"

"She has four other kids," Georgina admitted. "She probably doesn't want me around."

I thought of writing a woman a hefty check. Surely that would change her mind.

"Thank you for letting me stay with you," Georgina said in a small voice as we pulled up in front of the building. "I appreciate it, and you didn't have to."

"Of course I did," I cut in smoothly. "Now come on, let me show you to your room."

She stared in wonder at her surroundings as I took her up with the elevator. I gave her one of the kids guest rooms in the apartment, and she seemed delighted to be staying there, sending pangs of guilt through my mind. I wanted her to stay forever, but I could never be a foster parent. It would be too heartbreaking for me.

"I'll see you in the morning and we can talk about a more permanent solution," I told her, and she nodded, not meeting my eye. I lingered in the doorframe. "Are you hungry?"

She looked up, swallowing. "They didn't let me have dinner tonight because I misbehaved."

"Come on," I motioned for her to follow me, doing my best to ignore the rage I felt at how they'd treated her at that orphanage. "I'll make you my famous carbonara."

She giggled. "It's past midnight..."

"Doesn't matter, if you're hungry, you're hungry."

I led her into the kitchen and she sat on one of my bar stools while I made the food.

"You didn't decorate for Christmas," she said, glancing around the room.

"I was too sad," I admitted. "Christmas reminds me of... that woman I told you about."

She nodded, looking wiser than her eleven years. "Maybe you will have more Christmases with her."

"With your help, I just might." I presented her with a plate laden with pasta. "And voila. Bon appetit!"

She dug in with gusto, and I made a plate for myself too, digging into the meal. I liked having Georgina around. It made me feel less alone.

But I knew this wasn't a permanent solution. The girl deserved a real family, not a bachelor like me. I vowed to call her aunt the next day and figure out a place for her to stay. I owed that to her, at least.

CHAPTER 19

Amicia

11 months later

The next year was coming to an end. It had been almost a week since I'd left Grayson's apartment in tears. I'd waited until he fell asleep before sneaking out, leaving my gift for him under the Christmas tree we'd decorated together. Every day since then, I'd regretted my decision.

With a heavy sigh, I opened the doors to the theater. An all-too-familiar sight awaited me—dozens of girls vying for a single role, one that would likely slip through my fingers just as all the others had. But I was determined this time.

A year ago, Grayson Kline surprised me by keeping true to his promise. He paid for my time spent with him, and the money arrived in my bank account a few days after Christmas. At first, I wanted nothing to do with it. I marked it in my head as dirty money and refused to touch it.

For two months, the money remained untouched in my bank account. But after another failed audition and being close to thrown out of my newly rented apartment, I told myself I earned that money fair and square.

I used it to pay for a few months' rent in advance and some dance classes, which I excelled in. The money stayed in my account and I only took out the bare minimum needed to pay for my dance instructor.

Soon enough, I had completed years' worth of training in a few months' time. My trainer was Igor, a man who'd danced with the Bolshoi ballet in his youth and was now determined to make me a star. I did everything he said, and he told me I had a good shot of getting this audition. I could only hope he was right.

The role was for a production of Swan's Lake. I was auditioning for the main part, and though the chances of me scoring the lead role were small, I was more ready than ever to impress the people in that theater with my skills. I'd spent all night preparing, watching video after video of the choreography for the role. I was ready.

Holding my head up high, I waited in the seating area until my name was called. The people running the audition luckily didn't look familiar this time, and the woman sitting in the middle seat behind a long conference table gave me an encouraging smile. *I could do this.*

"Whenever you're ready," a man with an exaggerated moustache told me, and I nodded, allowing myself to close my eyes and count to three before I nodded to the pianist. The notes carried me into a dance I'd rehearsed for. I was good, but I didn't know whether it would be enough. It hadn't been so far.

Still, I gave it my all, twisting and turning on the stage until the song turned to its crescendo. Right there, in the most frantic moment, I stumbled. I felt a collective gasp go through the judging committee as I fell to the floor. Tears of humiliation burned my eyes, but I forced myself to lift my head and smile as if nothing had happened. I kept dancing, and I gave it my all.

Once I was finished, I bowed for the committee with a bright smile on my face. They clapped loudly; their faces enthusiastic as they gave me some praise as well as constructive criticism on my performance.

"Can you wait for us, maybe an hour or two while we see the rest of the applicants?" the man with the moustache asked, and I was all too eager to nod in agreement. I'd never been asked to stay after an audition, and I took it as a sign of good things to come.

Back in the waiting area, I nervously folded my hands in my lap. The minutes ticked by painfully slowly, and even though I tried to force myself to think of the audition, there was only one thing—one *man*—on my mind. Grayson Kline.

I missed him, though I hated admitting it. But he was gone for good, and that had been my decision—to cut him out of my life after I'd found out what he'd had his business associate do to Margaret. I couldn't be with a man like that. A man who killed people.

Still, a part of me was eager to run back into his arms. I wanted him. I missed his heated touch, the way he'd kissed me, the way he fucked me and made love to me and made me feel whole for the first time in my life. But my own morality was getting in the way, a painful reminder that he was a bad man that had no business being in my life. I couldn't be with Grayson. I shouldn't forgive him for what he'd done.

So why was I still yearning for him? Why was every waking moment spent thinking about the man who'd changed the course of my life forever? Why had fate been so cruel to throw me in his lap when we both knew we could never be together?

I swallowed the lump in my throat just as someone called out my name.

"Amicia Romano?"

"Yes?" I stood up, wiping my eyes before following the coordinator into the main room. Nerves were getting the best of me, and to top it all off, my heart was breaking into pieces, knowing Grayson and I were well and truly over.

"Thank you for waiting, Miss Romano," the man with the moustache said kindly, pointing for me to stand before them. "We were impressed by your technique and eagerness to learn more. While we cannot offer you the lead role in the ballet this time, we would be honored if you played Odile in this production. You will only appear in one act, but it should be a good starting point for you, should you consider accepting our offer."

I was too gobsmacked to say anything. I just stared at them, making the man chuckle as he waited for my reply. Finally, my speech returned, and I stuttered, "Are you sure?"

"Yes, we're quite certain," he said with a friendly smile. "You've impressed us here tonight. Somehow, you managed to even make your fall look graceful."

I laughed, tears finally spilling down my cheeks as I thanked them one by one profusely. They gave me some further instructions for the production, and I left the room with a bright smile and a sunny outlook on my future. Still, the thought of Grayson prevailed in my mind. *How happy could I truly be if I wasn't with the man I loved?*

I shook my head to get the thought out. I couldn't think of that, couldn't allow my feelings clouding my judgement. I'd left him for good reason, and he'd paid for the time I'd spent with him, just like he'd promised he would. It was well and truly over.

It was past nine p.m. as I made my way home through the dark streets. There was a flickering light pole in the middle of the street, and just like a couple of days prior, soft little snowflakes drifted from the sky, slowly melting on my cheeks. I should have been happy, but instead I felt alone and broken. There was nobody to share the victory with.

Since my first and last botched date, I hadn't gone out with anyone. Instead, I chose to focus on my dancing, improving my technique until nobody could deny it was perfect. And still, every night, I found myself thinking about Grayson. Wondering whether I'd made a mistake when I left, whether he missed me as much as I missed him. Whether he'd take me back.

Those moments ended in tears and long nights of fitful sleep. Fact of the matter was, Grayson had never reached out to me in the eleven months we'd spent apart. For him, we were done.

As I was making my way down the deserted street a couple of blocks down from the theater, the lights flickered on and off above me, and I looked up at them with a worried expression. *How ominous.*

I'd reached the end of the street when the lights flickered again, this time turning off completely. My breath caught in my throat as I heard movement behind me, adrenaline instantly taking over and preparing me for the intruder that touched my shoulder, prompting me to whip around in a defensive position.

"Don't touch me!" I snarled, ready to hit the intruder until my eyes zeroed in on the dark, tall figure before me. "What the..."

"Hello, Kitty."

Grayson's deep voice was like music to my ears, and I whimpered out loud when I heard him speak. The man instantly made me feel dizzy, his mere presence making my knees go weak.

"What are you doing here?" I asked, nervously looking over my shoulder. The streetlights were still out, the dark street illuminated by nothing but the moon. "How did you find me?"

"You should know by now I'll always keep an eye on you," Grayson told me, sending shivers down my spine.

"What do you w-want?" I managed.

"I'll get to that in a second." He gave me his winning smirk, making my stomach flutter with butterflies. "But first, Amicia, I need to know. Do you want me to leave you alone? Because if you do, if you really do, all you need is to say it right now, and I won't bother you again. Do you understand?"

I swallowed the lump in my throat, considering his question. But there had only ever been one answer.

"I don't want you to leave me alone," I admitted in a broken whisper.

"Good," Grayson grinned. He clicked his fingers together then, and suddenly, the street lit up again. My eyes opened in wonder as a group of carolers, kids in their pre-teens, arrived from around the corner, singing Holy Night.

"What is this?" I whispered, my eyes dancing between the man I loved and the group of children. One girl stood out, not older than eleven, with midnight black-blue hair and sparkling grey eyes.

"They're part of a charity I sponsor," Grayson explained. "I pay for each of their scholarships to a music school. There's others, too. Dancers. Performers. Actors."

"You never told me about this," I mumbled, looking up into his eyes and feeling the familiar rush of heat between my legs as our gazes locked.

"It's a new thing I'm doing," he said smoothly. "In your honor, Amicia. And I'd like you to head the program. To select the winners for the scholarship yourself."

"Well, it might interfere with the job I just got," I said, finally relaxing a little.

"Back at *Le Cabaret*?" Grayson inquired.

I shook my head. "No. I got a role in Swan Lake as Odile. The production begins in four weeks."

"Oh, Kitty. You must be thrilled." His eyes burned bright as they met mine and I fought the urge to beg him to take me back. To forget everything bad that had happened between us and just accept me the way I was, wanting to be his, wanting to be with him forever. "We'll have to celebrate."

"Oh?" I asked lamely, but Grayson merely gave me a knowing smile. The carolers came to a stop behind him, still singing the well-known tune that would forever remind me of that moment. My eyes widened as the man of my dreams slid down, resting on one knee as he looked up at me. "W-What are you doing, Sir?"

"I'm asking you to reconsider," he said firmly. "I've done bad things, Amicia. I... I want to spend the rest of my life atoning for them, with you by my side. I can't—won't—live without you. You've changed me in the twenty-four days we spent together. You've made me a better man. And I want to spend the rest of my life with you by my side, learning to be a better person, and owning up for my mistakes."

"So what are you saying?" My voice was embarrassingly shaky, and I swallowed the lump in my throat as I stared at him.

"I'm saying I want to marry you," he went on smoothly, opening the red velvet box that had materialized in his hand. A huge, solitaire diamond stared at me from a simple white gold band. "And this is the first, and last time I'm ever going to do this. I want you to be mine, forever. I want you by my side."

"But I'm no one," I said. "I'm a cabaret dancer... I'm... I'm going to embarrass you."

"You couldn't embarrass me if you tried," he said with a

smooth smirk. "But I want to spend the rest of my life being a better man for you, Amicia. Now, will you help an old man and tell me I can get off my knees? Will you marry me, my sweet Kitty?"

I wanted to consider his offer. I wanted to make him work for it. But there was really only one answer I could give him.

"Yes," I whispered.

He stood up, slipping the ring on my finger. I couldn't get the grin off my face, and as our eyes met again, my heart pounded with the knowledge of what I'd just done. It was foolish. It was too fast. Yet I'd never been surer of any decision I'd ever made than right there, at that moment.

Grayson embraced me, his strong arms holding my shaking body still as his lips found mine.

"I'm sorry," he whispered against my mouth.

And even though the words were final, it was only the beginning of our story.

CHAPTER 20

Grayson

It was our first Christmas together since Amicia had accepted my marriage proposal, and the first Christmas I was excited for. I had fun with her the first year, but this time around, I wouldn't let anything stand in my way of enjoying my Christmas captive to the full of her capabilities.

On Christmas Eve, we had dinner together and toasted to our upcoming marriage. Amicia was all smiles and I found it impossible to wipe the grin off my face. I told myself we both deserved this. Some happiness in a world of darkness, some light shining through the night. And yet I knew there was a conversation we had to have before my conscience could rest easily. And as

Amicia set down her glass of red wine, I cleared my throat and began to speak.

"Shall we talk about Margaret?"

Her face fell in an instant, and I wanted to regret my words, but I knew we had to talk about this.

"Do we have to?" Amicia asked softly.

"We do." I nodded. "I know how much her death hurt you, and that you still blame yourself for it. But that ends today."

"Oh?" She raised her brows at me. "What do you mean?"

"She died because of the debt," I went on. "And you're not going to blame yourself for that anymore. She took that money from you, didn't she?"

Amicia swallowed before nodding. "But that doesn't excuse what I did."

"You did nothing wrong, and I accept the full responsibility for her death," I went on. "But Amicia, you have to stop blaming yourself. She was a mean woman. She beat you and took things away from you. She stole years of your life, years that you can never have back. But you know what?"

"What?" she whispered.

"In a way, I'm grateful," I muttered. "Because without that old witch, we never would have met, and you wouldn't have become my Christmas captive."

She smiled reluctantly. "I wasn't a very good captive. I was more than willing to stay with you."

"If you hadn't been, I would've kept you anyway." My eyes glittered with desire as I drank her in. Amicia looked stunning in a midnight blue, jewel-toned velvet dress. Her hair was pinned up, with some dark tendrils escaping the chignon and framing her beautiful face. "Now, Amicia, are you ready for the real fun to begin?"

Curiosity sparkled in her eyes. "What did you have in mind?"

"Come to the playroom and find out." I set down my napkin, winking at her. "Meet you there in ten minutes. Strip down to your lingerie and put on some heels. There's a surprise waiting for you in the walk-in closet."

She clapped her hands together with excitement like a happy little girl. "I'll see you soon, Sir."

I went straight to the playroom, a smile playing on my lips as I imagined her opening the closet and seeing what I'd done for her. My employees had filled the wardrobe just for her. Beautiful dresses, expensive shoes, designer bags and fine jewelry completed the room. I couldn't wait to hear what Amicia thought.

Moments later, there was a knock on the door and Amicia entered with a wide smile on her lips. "I can't believe you did that for me, Sir."

"You deserve it," I told her. "And I like the heels you picked."

She put her foot forward, showing off a pair of tall Jimmy Choo mules with a diamond-encrusted strap, in the same blue velvet as her dress had been earlier. She wore a midnight blue lingerie ensemble complete with a garter belt and midnight black stockings, and I couldn't take my eyes off her.

"Come here," I beckoned her, and she came closer, standing in front of me so I could admire her ensemble up close.

"Oh, Sir!" She glanced up and smiled. "Did you know we were standing under mistletoe?"

"How appropriate," I grinned.

"We have to kiss."

"Yes, we do. Give me a moment." I reached up and pried the mistletoe off its red ribbon before holding it above my hips. "Looks like you'll have to kiss something other than my lips tonight, Kitty..."

She smiled mischievously and got on her knees, eyes sparkling with desire. "If you're so eager to have me suck your cock again, Sir, all you need to do is ask..."

"I prefer when you beg," I growled as she undid the zipper of my pants and brought out my already hard cock. "Fuck, Kitty. You better put it in your mouth."

"Of course, Sir," she purred, looking right into my eyes as she swirled her tongue over my tip. I groaned, hands going into her hair and wrapping in the strands of dark brown silk. "Like this?"

"Keep going," I grunted. "Keep fucking going."

I held the mistletoe above her as she began working my cock. Due to Kai's frequent check-ups, I knew she hadn't been with anyone else during our year apart—just like I hadn't. But it didn't seem to diminish her ability to suck cock like a pro. She worked me with her mouth and tongue, bringing me so close my cock throbbed between her full lips almost painfully.

"Are you going to come, Sir?" Amicia asked, sweetly batting her lashes. "Don't you want to come inside me?"

"Not tonight, Kitty," I grunted. "Tonight, you're going to eat it..."

She smiled and kept licking, working my cock until it stood upright, ready to unload in her waiting mouth.

"I'm hungry, Sir," she purred. "Please feed me..."

"Not yet," I muttered even though it was getting impossible to hold back with the way her tongue swirled around my slit, demanding I give in to her demands.

"Stop." I uttered the word with trouble, not really wanting her to stop sucking but eager to move on with the next part of our evening.

She sat back on her feet, eyes staring up at me. "Why, Sir? Did I do something wrong?"

"Not at all," I smiled. "But you'll still get spanked today. Not because you did something wrong, but because I want to."

"But I didn't misbehave!"

"I told you, it's for my pleasure. And yours too, if you're a good girl." I laughed out loud at her little pout. "Now be a good girl."

I walked over to the Chesterfield sofa and patted my knee after zipping up my pants. "Come here, Kitty. Right over my lap."

She pouted a bit more, but I could tell she wasn't able to resist. Finally, she crawled closer, raising herself and resting her body over my knees. Her tight, juicy little ass was presented to me, her skin pale ivory. The perfect canvas for the red handprints I'd put all over her complexion.

"Beg me to spank you," I muttered.

"Why?" She turned to face me, upset eyes staring into mine.

"Because I said so. Because you love it. Because you want to please me, Kitty."

"Sir..."

"Do as you're told if you want my cum tonight."

She pouted, her lips pouting without any words coming out. But finally, she whispered, "Please Sir, will you spank my ass for your pleasure?"

"Gladly, Kitty." I rained slap after slap against her tender backside. At first, she mewled in protest, glaring at me, but soon enough, her yelps turned into moans of pleasure and she started arching her back, bringing her tight ass closer and closer to my punishing hand.

I spanked her until she was moaning my name, soft whispers begging for more attention to her needy little cunt. I knew I couldn't keep her like that forever—she was eager for me to kiss her, to give her pleasure, not just mix it with pain.

"You've been a good girl, Kitty," I finally muttered, pulling her into my lap. She curled up against my chest and I found myself cherishing the moment of closeness. "Are you ready for your prize?"

"Yes, Sir," she whispered, curling up close against me. "What's my prize?"

I pointed to a gold bar cart in the corner of the room where an opaque cloche was covering a plate. "Why don't you open it and see."

Excitedly and with newfound energy, Amicia picked herself up from my lap and ran to the bar cart. She lifted up the cloche, coming face-to-face with a plate of macadamia and white chocolate cookies.

"Cookies?" She raised her eyebrows, eyes glowing with surprise. "For me or for Santa?"

I laughed out loud. "For you, my darling. But we need to add something to it first, don't you think?"

Realization dawned on her and she laughed out loud. She brought the plate closer and set it down on the coffee table. The still-warm cookies' scent wafted up into the room, creating the perfect Christmas atmosphere.

"Take my cock out again," I muttered, and my Kitty rushed to do as she was told, pulling my cock free of the pants I was wearing. "Good girl. I want your hands today. You can use your mouth to help you, but don't let me come down your throat."

She started working my cock, her silky soft hands palming me closer and closer to an orgasm.

I knew I would get too close soon enough, especially when her mouth joined the work she was doing with her hands, licking, sucking, bringing me so very close I wanted to burst right down her throat and say fuck it to all my previous instructions.

But I couldn't. I had a special plan for my load that night, so I pulled out of her mouth gently.

"Ah ah ah, Kitty," I reminded her. "Use your hands now. Look up at me when you do."

Her pillow-soft palms both wrapped around my shaft, jerking

as she moaned my name, eyes locked with mine. I groaned, knowing I was getting dangerously close to a release a part of me wanted to prolong as much as I possibly could. But I knew I couldn't, not with the way her fingers deftly wrapped around me, jerking, bringing me so very close I groaned, tugging on her hair to slow her down.

"Get the cookies," I grunted. "Now."

She took the plate in one of her hands, seemingly realizing what I wanted her to do. Her eyes shone brightly as she jerked me with one hand and balanced the cookies beneath me with the other. Soon enough, I couldn't hold back a second longer.

I groaned her name in time with my release. Hot ropes of cum shot out of my cock, landing on the cookies like perfect buttercream frosting.

"Yummy," Amicia laughed, licking her lips and kissing the remainder of cum off my cock, cleaning my diligently. I didn't even have to tell her to eat up. She raised the cookie to her lips herself, enjoying the taste of sweetness mixing with my own gift for her as she ate them one by one.

I took the time to calm down from my orgasm, watching her with pure pleasure. She was the only woman I'd ever met who treated my cum like the gift it was.

"My dirty girl," I grinned, running my fingers through her dark hair that had long since come undone from its tight updo. She looked perfect like this, disheveled and yet so very beautiful in her natural state. Her cheeks were reddened, her lips glowing from and her eyes glittering as she licked her mouth. Amicia's little tongue darted between her lips and licked every little trace of my cum off. She groaned with pleasure. "You made me so happy today, Kitty. Did you like your little Christmas treat?"

"I loved it, Sir," she purred with pleasure. "Was I a good girl for you?"

"The best. You're most certainly on Santa's nice list this year, my darling."

"Good," she smiled mischievously. "Maybe tomorrow I can get on the naughty one..."

I laughed out loud. "You want to get punished?"

"If it's with you," she said, licking her fingers with gusto. "I want it all..."

EPILOGUE

Amicia

1 year later

"Here Kitty, Kitty..."

I crawled toward him on all fours. Grayson's eyes burned bright with want as he saw me, and he petted my head as I came to rest on the pillow next to him, my knees sinking into the soft, plushy fabric.

"What a good girl you are. Are you ready for your present?" he asked, giving me an affectionate smile as he tugged on my long dark locks.

"Yes, Master," I whispered. The word still felt delicious

coming from my lips—forbidden, yet so very right for our relationship. I'd been calling him Master for almost a full year now, but he still hadn't collared me. I had a feeling he had a special plan for that, though I never dared to ask.

The past year has been life changing. The day he proposed to me, Grayson took me back home to his penthouse. I never went back to my apartment after that. He had someone clear it out and bring me some mementos I'd left over, but from that New Year's Eve, I belonged to him fully. The knowledge that I wasn't just his beloved wife, but also his most prized possession, filled me with happiness and eagerness to please my Master for the rest of my life. I hadn't just found my soulmate in Grayson—I'd found the thing that had been missing from my life all along. And in kneeling for my Master, I had found myself.

"How pretty you look tonight," he muttered as he caressed my cheek. "Go on, then. Bring over that square box under the tree, I want to see you open it. And don't get off your knees. I want to see you crawl some more, Kitty."

I smiled, crawling to the tree, and swaying my ass from side to side so he could get a good look at me. I picked the box up, standing up and placing it in Grayson's lap, barely able to hold back the smile playing on my lips.

"Don't you want to open it, Kitty?" he asked in a low growl.

"Yes, Master."

"Then ask for permission."

"Can I open it?" I whispered.

"Ask properly, Kitty." He pinched my nipple through the blouse I was wearing, making me whimper with need. "Go on, give it another go."

"Please, Master... *may* I open it?" I tried again.

"Yes, Kitty, you may." He kissed my cheek as he handed me the box, a mischievous grin playing on his lips.

I tore through the snowflake printed wrapping paper and gasped when I saw the midnight blue velvet jewelry box beneath the paper. "What's this, Master?"

"You'll have to open it and see."

With trembling fingers, I gently lifted the lid of the box, gasping when I saw what was inside. A gorgeous gold collar lay atop the fabric, with the sweetest little bell dangling from the front.

"A pretty collar for a pretty Kitty," Grayson told me with an affectionate smile, sweeping my hair off my neck. "Let me put it on you?"

"Yes, Master," I breathed. "Please..."

His fingers felt cool against my skin as he put the collar in place. When I felt the lock clicking, it was as if everything came together. Brimming with happiness, I shared a special smile with Grayson that made me tingle.

"All mine now, Kitty," he said. "I don't want you to take it off again."

"Never," I whispered as he pressed a firm kiss against my mouth. "I want everyone to know I belong to you. Thank you, Master."

He deepened our kiss, the raw passion he felt for me obvious from the way his lips melded against mine, claiming me as his time and time again.

"What's on the agenda today?" he finally asked when I pulled back.

"I have rehearsals in two hours, and the performance tonight at eight," I explained. "Will I see you in the audience tonight?"

"You have to ask?" he grinned at me. "There's no chance I'd miss your first performance, Kitty. You'll make a wonderful Odile. I'm sure you'll make me very proud."

"But..." I bit my bottom lip, giving him a hopeful look. "I

want to do something else first."

"What's that?" he asked.

"I wanted to invite Georgie over to lunch," I suggested. "We have something we want to ask you."

"Oh?" Grayson raised his brows in amusement. "And what might the two of you be planning, Kitty?"

"You'll have to wait and see." I gave him a mysterious smile, my heart pounding in expectation.

Georgina or Georgie as we liked to call her, was the pretty young girl with jet black hair who'd been part of the group of carolers singing to me when Grayson proposed. She was one of the beneficiaries of Grayson's scholarship, and an incredibly talented singer. I was close with a lot of the children Grayson sponsored, but sweet little Georgie had a special place in my heart.

Hopefully, Grayson felt the same way. I'd find out soon enough.

***

"Will you pass the green bean casserole?"

Georgie handed me the dish with a bright smile on her face. She looked hopeful, her pale cheeks aglow with embarrassment as she glanced at Grayson. She was always so respectful around him, but Grayson liked to tease her and joke around with her, making her a little more comfortable in his company.

"We had something we wanted to ask you, Grayson," I went on, my eyes sparkling as they met my husband's.

"Oh?" he asked, a smile playing on his lips. A part of me was sure he already knew what I was going to say, but still, my heart sped up as my nerves got the best of me. "Well, ask away, my pretty ladies. I would love to know."

I touched my collar self-consciously, but the jingle of the

little bell on it reminded me that everything would be okay.

"Well, as you know," Georgie spoke up, her voice decidedly formal. "I'm staying with my auntie right now while my mom gets... better."

Grayson nodded, shooting me a long look. We both knew Georgie's mom wasn't coming back, though the little girl hadn't quite accepted it yet. "Go on, Georgina."

"Auntie Tracie has her hands full," she went on softly. "And Amicia, well... she suggested maybe I could stay with you for a little while."

"Just a little while?" Grayson teased her; his eyes glowing bright. "Or would you like to stay longer, maybe?"

I could tell Georgie was battling with what she thought was polite, and what she really wanted to say.

"It's okay," I said, gently squeezing her hand. "You can be honest."

"I suppose..." She bit her lip self-consciously. "As long as you'll have me..."

"Well, my dear, that will be a very long time," Grayson grinned. "And I had a feeling this question was coming, so I took it upon myself to arrange something already. I hope you ladies don't mind."

"Oh?" I asked, giving him a concerned look. "What have you arranged?"

"I took it upon myself to arrange some papers for Georgie," he went on, getting up and pulling out a folder from the bookcase in the dining room. "There were some... complications... but I sorted it out."

He gave me a sly grin. Sometimes his strange business practices came in handy, and even I ended up being grateful for the way he did things.

"What's this?" Georgie asked carefully as he slid the papers over to her.

"Adoption papers," Grayson said firmly. "Your aunt has already signed them."

I could see the small look of disappointment on Georgie's face, but it was gone in an instant, her hand trembling as she picked up the pen. "What does it mean if I sign them? That I get to stay with you... for a long time?"

"Forever." Grayson grinned. "Or as long as you like."

"Where do I sign?" she asked, making me tear up.

"Right here. But there's one other requirement," Grayson spoke up.

"What's that?"

"You can't call me Mr. Kline anymore," Grayson teased her.

Georgie gave him a tentative smile, whispering, "What do I call you then?"

"Well, whatever you want," my husband told her, giving me his winning smile. "Grayson. Definitely not Sir. If you want... I suppose you could even call me Dad."

"Dad." Georgie tested the name out on her lips. "I like that."

Grayson reached for my hand across the table and I did my best to hide the happy tears fighting their way onto my face.

"I like it very much, too," he told her, squeezing my hand under the table.

"We might have another surprise for you," I said a moment later.

"Oh?" Grayson's eyes sparkled in the candlelit room. "What's that, darling?"

I rested my trembling hand on my stomach as I said, "Georgie isn't the only new girl in your life."

His eyes grew wider and wider as he stared at me. "Are you saying..."

"I'm pregnant." I smiled shyly, still unused to those strange words coming from my lips. Ever since the doctor told me, I'd been worried about Grayson's reaction. But seeing him then, I never should have worried at all.

He stood up, kneeling in front of me.

"Are you going to propose again?" I teased him, giggling to hide the emotions hidden by my laugh.

"You're already mine, aren't you?" he spoke up gruffly. The joy I'd made him feel was obvious though, and we smiled at one another when a flash blinded us. We both looked up to find Georgie with an old-fashioned camera, giggling as a Polaroid of our first real Christmas together developed.

"Don't mind me," she smiled wide. "I just wanted to start one of many memories we'll have together."

"So we shall," Grayson grinned, admiring me with his eyes. "You've made me the happiest man alive, Amicia. I didn't know it was possible to be this happy."

"Neither did I," I whispered, giving him an affectionate smile as Georgie proudly presented me with a perfect Christmas shot of our new family.

Outside, the snow fell softly, covering London in a white, thick coat of promises. I smiled as my husband laughed with our newly adopted little girl, my hand resting protectively on my stomach.

This year, I certainly would have a jolly Christmas.

Isabella Starling